BITE THE BULLET OR BITE ME ANYWAYS

Waroon Maihra

© Waroon Maihra 2019

All rights reserved

All rights reserved by author. No part of this publication may be reproduced, stored in a retrieval system or transmitted in any form or by any means, electronic, mechanical, photocopying, recording or otherwise, without the prior permission of the author.

Although every precaution has been taken to verify the accuracy of the information contained herein, the author and publisher assume no responsibility for any errors or omissions. No liability is assumed for damages that may result from the use of information contained within.

First Published in November 2019

ISBN: 978-93-5347-948-0

BLUE ROSE PUBLISHERS
www.bluerosepublishers.com
info@bluerosepublishers.com
+91 8882 898 898

Cover Design:
Pallavi Porwal

Typographic Design:
Namrata Saini

Distributed by: Blue Rose, Amazon, Flipkart, Shopclues

"I'm writing my story so that others might see fragments of themselves." - *Lena Waithe*

Each one of us has an instinct to rise, like a flame of the lamp. Let's nurture this instinct." - *Narendra Modi*

A year from now you will wish you had started today.
- *Karen Lamb*

The greatest mistake you can make in life is to be continually fearing you will make one." - *Elbert Hubbard*

"Nothing is worth more than laughter. It is strength to laugh and to abandon oneself, to be light. Tragedy is the most ridiculous thing." - *Frida Kalho*

आत्मानं सततं ज्ञात्वा कालं नय महामते / प्रारब्धमखिलं भुञ्जन्नोद्वेगं कर्तुमर्हसि // - *Bhagavat Gita*

कभी ज़िन्दगी से इश्क़ करके देख ... ऐसा आशिक बानायगी .. जन्नत भी यहीं और इबादत भी यहीं - *Varun Anita Mehra*

La vida no tiene que ser perfecta para ser hermosa
- *Anoymous*

Credits

Anita Mehra
For being the force for my shaping.

Ria Kapoor
For letting me pen it down.

Kunal Kapoor
You have been a gentleman and a true family man... A reason why I could feel it the way I have.

Anuj Sharma
For everything you got me... Like a deer!!! I hope you are more fair to yourself alongwith being fair to others!! Thank you for letting me use your clicks and thoughts!!! Love

Gunjan Ramchandani
Like a positive stimulation, you have been my partner in crime, and I value everything we have spoken and done. Unadulterated friendship!! Thank You for that.!!

Sadhil Kapoor
For letting me use your clicks... for bringing the love to family.

Deepak Mehra
We are different but we value the relationship. You have been selfless most of the time.

Kiran and Pranath Mehra
I miss you!! And irrespective I love you. Thank you!

Khwahish Kapoor
For letting me use your clicks… for bringing the love to family.

Trikhas
The silent and saner around!!! Love you and thank you!

Angie
For being a great source of influence … Sister from another Mister.. God bless u.

Sarita
I can now say with having had experienced that I owe you!!!

Parag
Thank You for everything.

Rahool
Bud!!! You are truly a friends' friend!!

Ranjeet
You are my dilli-jaan dost!!! Thank You for being you and being a deep partner in thoughts.

Laung/Lachi
Love my babies!!

Tanya
My sister from another Mister! God bless u with love. Thank You.

Dhaarna
You have showered unconditional love to me and I truly value that

Shikha / Geetanjali
In the most important times of my life, you were there like a wall.

Mum and Dad
I will always be indebted to you.. Love You!!! The respect and care is unmatched!

Prakhar
For all the designs and selfless.

Nitin
For being honest and vulnerable

Diego, Frooti, Ivy, Lucy, Bianca
I love You!

Schnapps
You have made us a better human ... I love you baby!!!

About the Previous Book

"Truly awesome... It's a mixture of romance, suspense, excitement and lots more. The best part is its a series of short but awesome stories. And the poems are very visual and romantic. For someone as adventurous as the author he has done full justice to the book. And being the first book I hope there are more to come. A must read book specially for those who are romantic and visual. Afterall the author is truly a love guru in all aspects....Love it to the core. Thank you for giving us such an awesome book."

                                     - Reader on Amazon.com

"Soulfully deep yet simple, writer has done amazing job of penning every human emotion. Highly recommended for all"

— **Ranjeet Halder**

"We need more of these. It's super amazing."

— **Anjali Dogra**

"U had written it so beautifully....its so romantic & emotional tooo...got tears in my eyes while reading.....each & every word touched my soul....loads of love & wishes... Waiting for more to come 💘 ♡ 😍 💋"

— **Ria Kapoor**

Contents

It Just Happened	4
My Little Boi	37
Why Fly When You Own the Sky	39
Another Life Another Day	67
I Don't Want it Anyways	90
Apple Of Others Eyes; Kept the Doctor Away	92
The Yellow Silence	149
Leh'd On My Birthday	154
Mars Was Always on the List	174
Morning Blues	188
…And I Didn't Stop Loving Vegas	192
Not the Usual Way	207

Before you begin reading, here is what I would want you to immerse and walk down the memory lane. Answer the following questions for yourself?

QUESTION: What is on the TOP of your bucket list of TO DOs ?

QUESTION: Who would you most like to swap places with for a day?

QUESTION: If you were to start a company of yours, what would be the product?

QUESTION: What is that one moment that you won't trade off for anything?

QUESTION: What would you want to tell your own self 10 years from now?

QUESTION: If you were to relive a secret of yours, what would that be?

QUESTION: If you were to write one story in your life, what would that be about?

It Just Happened

Vyom was on his way to home and suddenly he got a text …. It was from a dating app and he couldn't resist … the guy looked cute and had sharp eyes … he asked for further information …. And realized that he was very far considering Vyom had reached his apartment.

Marlon insisted that he would like to meet and if he could get Vyom's contact number. Vyom texted the mobile phone number and the phone rang immediately.

"That was quick ahhaaa? Vyom mentioned. "Hi, This, is Marlon… I just called to inform you that I will be leaving in about 15 minutes and will call you when I am about to leave?"

Vyom felt a little strange for the guy sounded very naïve but wasn't naïve on the chat. He decided to go with the flow.

10 minutes later, he received a text that there was an important meeting that had come and Marlon could take another 1 hour. "Like every other man who chickens out and has the busiest life…." Vyom thought. And then his phone rang…. It was the same number.

"Hey hi…. I called in to let you know that I have a meeting that has come up and my boss won't set me free until he is done with the meeting so just wait for me …. Would you be comfortable to have me at your place late night?" Marlon said all of this in one go.

"Well… aaaah … am not sure what you mean coz its u who should be worried and not me for the late night…" Vyom was puzzled with Marlon's question for it didn't sound right to him.

"I said that coz I know some men may not be ok with the late-night stuff" Marlon responded.

"I got no problem.... You text me when you leave, and we take it from there ...." Vyom responded.

"Alight done deal.... I will let you know if I am coming or not .... If I go beyond 10.30pm then we can meet later.... I hope you ok with that? Marlon responded.

"Alright, I shall see you soon." Vyom bid good bye.

"Ciao" Marlon acknowledged.

10 minutes later, Marlon called again. " Please wait for me.... I really want to meet you. If I leave by 10:30pm, can I use your washroom to take shower... I really need it" Marlon said.

"Well sure and hell ya ... you got to use the washroom after work." Vyom responded.

He ran into the room and began cleaning the house... just incase the guy shows up.

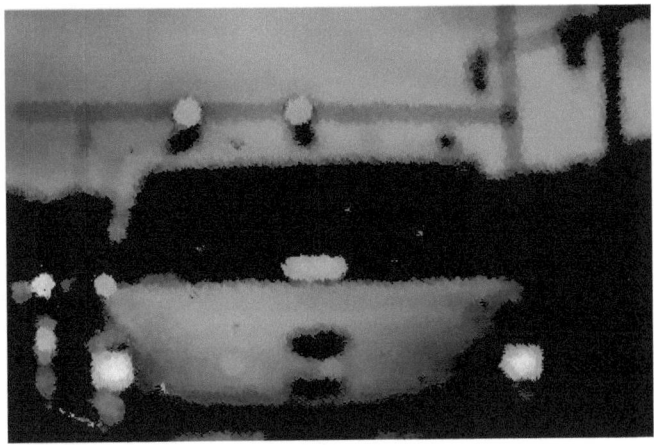

After 1-hour Vyom thought that the guy wasn't gonna show and began setting up the bed for the night.

He picked up the utensils, cleaned the kitchen and started fixing his bed while the music was on. "I could plan a movie late night" Vyom began checking various options online when suddenly the phone rang.

"Hey, listen…. I am leaving from here in about 5 minutes and will call you. The meeting got over soon so I should be there in about 30 minutes." Marlon mentioned.

Vyom replied "Well, that's fine. Comeover and call me when you are closeby."

45 minutes had passed and there was no response. Vyom kept looking at the clock and was almost giving up … rather decided to wrap up the day and the phone rang…

"Hey, I am around your place… can you guide me?" Marlon called.

Vyom looked down from the balcony and saw the guy. He looked very thin…. Had a beard and a very different walk…. "Did I make the right decision?" Vyom questioned but then decided to go with the flow.

They both shook hands and checked out eachother. Vyom had worn a nice pyjama for he was almost prepared to snooze off.

Marlon entered the house and was spellbound. The house was very well done…. It had beautiful paintings and quotations on the call. The lights were dimmer.

Vyom was very confused…. He kept looking for reasons to stay in the kitchen and Marlon seemed too fast and forward to him. He asked for a towel so that he can get ready. Vyom continued being in the kitchen.

Vyom felt a little strange for it wasn't easy for him to have someone in his apartment.

"How do you manage the house? You stay alone and you have managed it really well" Marlon asked.

"I enjoy doing the household chores and that destresses me so …yep I do invest time in setting it up" Vyom responded.

"Well I am sure.... Look at yourself.... You look great .... I mean I can't even imagine you to come and visit my place for you would hate it ...its in a mess and has stuff allover." Marlon said.

Vyom was grinning for he knew that he is a messy one himself but was ready to temporarily take the title of being OCD. "Well yes, I like cleanliness around me and I try and ensure that the place where I stay is clean and comfortable." Vyom inflated his own ego.

Marlon asked about Vyom and Vyom was a little apprehensive to share the details hence he lied all the time.

"Hey, before I go to the shower.... Can you give me something to eat and maybe make coffee for both of us?" Marlon insisted.

Vyom was almost losing his patience. He wanted to be nice to him considering he had come back from work and Marlon's constant overreach made him forget his humanity concept.

"Well... I have some nachos and I can make you something to eat... Let me put up the coffee first. You get shower." Vyom smiled and responded.

After 5 minutes, Marlon came out of the shower and said that he will wait for the bucket to be filled.

"Hey Vyom... I am really hungry ... I didn't get time to eat anything the entire day. If its ok, can you make some Maggie if you have ... sorry I might sound like crazy, but I am really hungry, and I want to eat something substantial." Marlon looked at Vyom and said.

"WOW.... Does he think am his waiter or what .... He is here for food??? .... Vyom, be nice to him. Poor boy has come from work and the least you could do is feed him." Vyom was juggling between his thoughts.

"I can make rice… I will quickly chop the veggies and make it." Vyom responded.

"aww… thank you… u must be mad at me but thank you so much." Marlon accompanied while Vyom was entering the kitchen.

"Why is he stalking me" the thought ran through Vyom's mind.

"Can I take shower while you make rice?" Vyom raised his eyebrows after listening to this.

The facial expression told Marlon that something is wrong… "Are you ok? I hope I am not pushing you through?" Marlon enquired smirkingly.

Vyom didn't have a choice for he wanted to let go off the time as soon as it can. "Sure, No problem, take your time!" Vyom said with some sense of sigh.

Marlon took 2 hours to bath and Vyom was done making rice and tea. Marlon stepped out of the washroom in the pyjamas. "Why would someone carry Pyjama to work and a T. Looks like he carries this everyday so that he could sleep around. He looks like a maniac. I am not going to let him stay longer." Vyom was visibly confused about him.

Vyom became suspicious. He raised his guards and began looking for the biggest knife in the kitchen.

Marlon served himself tea and rice. "Wow, its amazingly made, Vyom. Why don't you marry me?" Marlon asked.

Vyom looked at him and his pyjamas … "Why would you suddenly pop that question up?" Vyom asked.

"Well, you are good looking guy. You stay alone, you are romantic, you earn well, you make nice food and tea. You love to write poems, this is perfect!! "

"Yeah right!!" Vyom stopped his search for the hidden knife.

"Come sit close to me." Marlon asked Vyom. Vyom was very uncomfortable with Marlon's comfortably taking control of the house.

"So let me read your poems!! I can add a lot of emotions and recite poems." Marlon asked and Vyom agreed.

Marlon read Vyom's written poems with almost perfect sound. Vyom couldn't believe he wrote all this and Marlon couldn't stop gushing over that he was sitting with an 'author'.

" You know there is so much love in you ..so much romance... how come you are single?" Marlon asked Vyom.

"You don't want to hear my break up stories. They are not meant to be discussed. Besides you tell me about yourself!!" Vyom asked Marlon.

"Well, I work with an NGO sponsored by Norway and Netherland government to understand impact of world changes" Marlon mentioned while Vyom looked swayed with his international credentials.

"That sounds sexy." Vyom couldn't control.

"Well listen to me... Can you get me the left over rice. I am very hungry." Marlon asked Vyom.

"Its not easy, my boss eats my head to attend meeetings beyond my working hours. I have an old granny that I stay with and I need to take care of her. She is my life. I want to spend time with her but just don't get time. My sister is here and she has been helping me manage and take care of her. I come from Kolkata. I don't usually pop up like this after work but I didn't want to miss the chance to meet you." Marlon mentioned while Vyom looked displeased with the last sentence for he couldn't stop thinking about the pyjamas in the bag.

"Let me read the poems to you and spend time talking about the poems and their history" Marlon moved to a different topic very quickly. He read the poems and looked at Vyom while Vyom was telling the history and the deep meaning of the poems.

"I wrote the poems as my journey of life… How I felt. Romance can't be sane..it has to be wild and induldging… And I always believed…" Marlong pulled Vyom towards him while Vyom was talking about the poems and kissed him. Vyom was stunned. Marlon moved a little back, looked into Vyom's eyes and lips… Vyom was still shocked… "This is for the poet you are … for being you.." Marlon kissed Vyom again. Vyom felt the breath of Marlon closed to his lips and he began trembling for he couldn't figure out the series of events.

"I didn't see this coming so soon." Vyom couldn't stop thinking. Marlon asked Vyom to keep his head on his own shoulders. He held his hand and jumped over him to kiss him again. Vyom felt unseated … his hands pushing towards the floor to avoid being pushed… Marlon passionately kissed Vyom …. He bit Vyom while he became motionless. Marlon held his face in hands and kissed his eyes and nose. He lifted Vyom's upper lip with his lower lip.

Marlon asked if they could move to the bedroom. Vyom looked confused and unsure …. He got up and pulled Vyom up and moved to the bedroom.

Vyom was very surprised with the speed of events. Marlon slept over the bed and asked Vyom to keep his head on him and they began talking until Marlon realized that Vyom has gone off to sleep.

Marlon looked at Vyom, caressed his forehead and went to sleep.

He woke up 2 hours later and left while Vyom was sleeping. As the door closed, Vyom got up to hear and realized that Marlon had left. He checked his things around to confirm if Marlon took anything. And Marlon didn't say goodbye or anything and just left and nothing was missing from the house.

Vyom was very confused and locked the gate.

"SOMETIMES YOU MEET PEOPLE TO REMIND YOU ABOUT YOURSELF AND ALLOWS YOU TO INDULDGE IN LIFE"

My mind is just like birds... Some may say it's a cage in your arms but nobody knows I feel liberated and free in your arms

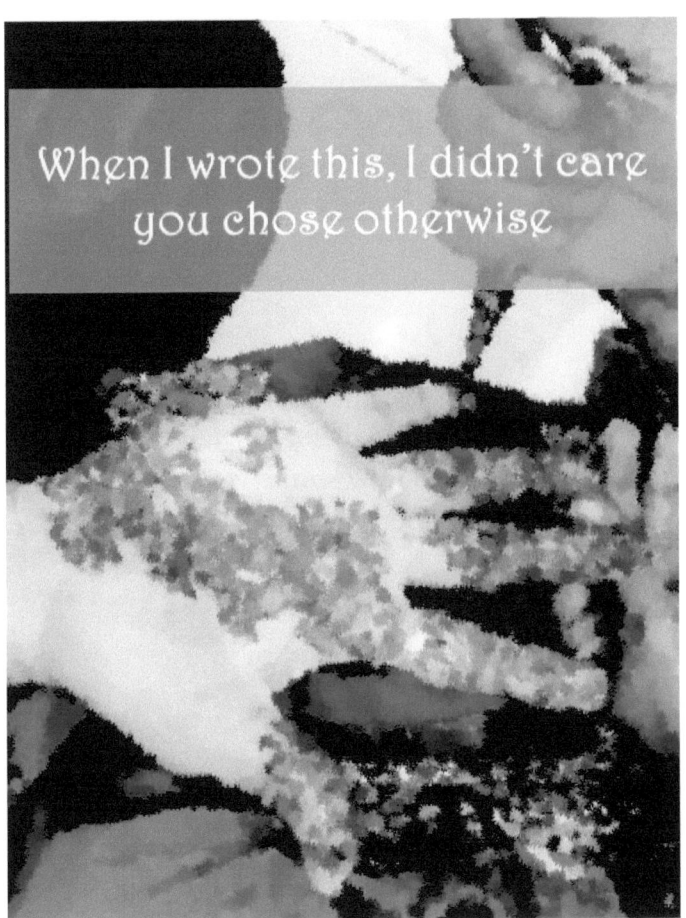

He asked if he is a storyteller;
He responded if he wants to hear one
or create one!

He promised him to never leave his hands;
When he lost his hand, he dropped his hand.

He told everyone about his first love for her
sister; She suddenly skipped the beat for
she had tried 35 years of marriage to
not let anyone know his truth

She didn't leave the bench at the station;
Her son had told her 3 days ago that he would
return in few minutes.

He thought of the promise that he won't sell his body and suddenly he heard the doorbell;
They had come.

He promised him that he will pay $50 for he
wanted to just feel a human touch;
The guy came and unzipped instead.

ए आशिक़ कभी गलती से करो तो सही

कभी उनकी **नज़रें** मिली कभी हमारी उनसे..
कभी उन्होंने देखा हमें कभी हमने देखा उनको
ऐसे ही रात हो गयी और वह आज फिर नहीं आये

She turned to cry for mercy in the dark;
What he saw was her sister begging his
friends to leave her while he was shooting all of it

Everyday his phone used to ring at 2pm when his father called, which he used to avoid; This day he realized that its 2pm when he cremated his father; No more calls.

She bagged the beauty pageant and the first thing she did was to eat Pizza.

He was told that he is just ok and he kept chasing them; The guy told him that he is sexy and wants him; he dumped him.

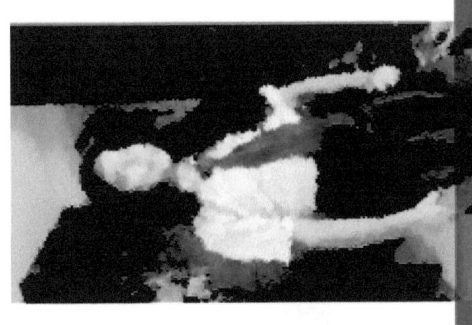

SO DON'T LET ANYONE DRAW YOUR SKY FOR THERE IS UNISERVSE BEYOND THE STARS!!!

AND THE BEST DELIGHTS OF THE LIFE ARE MEANT TO MAKE YOU FEEL HAPPY ABOUT YOURSELF!!!

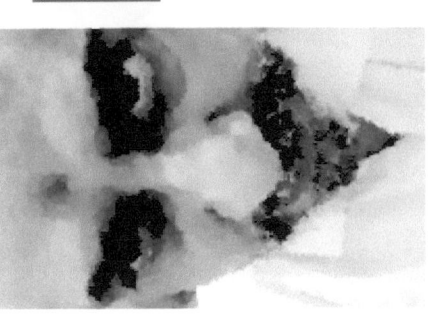

LIFE IS AN EXPERIMENT THAT DOESN'T FAIL... YOU LEARN AND MOVE ON!!

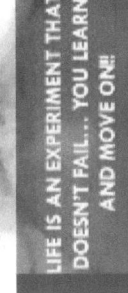

He asked her to remove her clothes; she caressed her tummy and said "I need to do this to get you in the world so close your eyes."

He told him that he didn't like sex all the time;
And then he was Active after every 2 hours
asking for vanilla sex and fucks.

He paid to stay in the old age home before
he gets too old in his lonely house.

She came out of hospital; Her father walked
out and thought of starting
to save money.

He told her not to be his mistress,
yet he opened the door for him to come.

He looked at his mehndi and said "Finally, I see a man putting mehndi, Now I won't be scared to put it on my hands!!!

My Little Boi

Little Boi…

Hey Little Boy

You will laugh out when you would think of me

And when you would wanna see those eyes

Don't have to go far

Look into your heart

For that's where you would find

Not my eyes but the ashes of my life

You always said that you are like sand …

Can't hold tight in my hands

Now try and hold me or my ashes

Even when your heart wants to just touch me

It will only give you my cries

Hey little boy

Let me tell you something new

You told me that whatever be the case

You would always be married to me

But I chose to ignore my instinct and trust your words

And now those words are sitting in the photos

Of broken promises and broken dreams

You made a sigh-filled exit

And you were supposed to be my side

When I decided to fight the battle

You robbed me of my soul

And then you tell me that you gave me my world

I didn't ask for this, little boy

I know I begged and howled to stop you

And I cried but you walked away

You killed me and made me do things I didn't think

I would ever give up my soul and do

Hey little boy

Don't forget when you first met me

Shook my hands when you first saw

I saw you in your yellow shirt and your nerdy glass

My heart did something for it knew what was coming

But my head did the trick and told me to stay away

7 months of chase crashed in 4 months of tides

What love were you building in the 4 years that couldn't stand the wides

Don't worry

You have the ashes with you

Now try and save them for that's all there with you!!

Why fly When you Own the Sky

Building Wings and Claws

Anita was a cute little girl who lived in a small town close to the countryside. Due to the ongoing war between the two nations, the families were required to stay in the house under blackout during the night. But that didn't stop Anita to chase her desires... At least she could chase them without the desire to achieve them.

Bravery and innocence made her unique. She was very fond of the mystic planes in the air and that night, the sounds of jets were powerful enough to drive her to the terrace; Like a butterfly, she flew to get a glimpse of the jets in the air; jeopardizing and breaking the rules.

Her mother ran after her to stop but Anita ran faster until a bucket hit her foot and she fell with her forehead hitting the floor. The sound was so loud that her mother thought she jumped off the terrace; Poor woman could hardly see anything, and she screamed.

"Maa, quiet. The enemy country will know. Now come here and save me" Anita screamed in low voice. Her mother had a sigh of relief and took her down. The house had 4 floors; It was a cozy small set up. When she came down, the mother saw her forehead bleeding. Her mother panicked but didn't know what to do for her mother was scared to step out. She called the family doctor for help; The doctor was close family friend and came running to check.

"Nothing, I have put the bandage and done some stitches … Not a big deal but she has to be careful now… She could have lost her eyesight but thank god; nothing fatal happened There is just one thing though, her eye and the eyebrow will have this mark (pointing towards it) for life until miraculously something makes it normal. And yes, she cannot have ice-creams for she could lose her eyesight." The doctor said.

Doctor Khanna knew Anita's madness for ice-creams, so he added up to tease her. "I don't care if I lose my eyesight. I can't lose the sight to eat the ice-cream." Anita hooked onto that joke.

Nobody knew that she will be called cursed with that mark.

Her full of life and mischievous mind didn't deter her and she continued to do things she enjoyed.

Anita was famous amongst her cousins as the "thug" of the group … while she kept a lot of her desires within, for she knew she wouldn't be allowed to do things. She wanted to learn dancing and singing but her over traditional parents didn't support the idea. A girl called as the bird with the wings and claws, she was known for her madness in the family.

From dancing under shower, singing songs under quilt, reading newspaper and reading it out loud for everyone, she liked everything in her control. Her father knew she wasn't the usual girl who would sit but his terror was enough for her to hide things and do them only in his absence. Such was Anita and her tales.

On a full moon day, Anita wanted to drink tea but her sister didn't let her and instead drank her share. Anita was angry and decided to avenge. Everyone decided to sleep on the terrace for the window was cool and breezy; Anita decided to sleep with her sister on the old traditional bed which made sound anyways.

In the middle of the night, she opened her eyes to see everyone sleeping when she decided to avenge; She went underneath the bed, tied the hair of her sister with no sound whatsoever and came back, holding her pillow to press it on her sister's face. As she was about to do that, her father woke up. Anita got scared and moved underneath the bed to save herself. Her mother and father left the terrace to sleep in the room. And while she saw them leaving, she grinned with evil thoughts and stood up, on the bed and began jumping on her sister's tummy. Her sister's face was covered with a pillow and Anita was laughing with the adrenaline rush to get back to her sister. From that night she was told to sleep alone, and Anita saw her victory for she had a room to herself. She didn't know this, but she was preparing herself to win over all odds in life in all situations.

All Odds are even

At 15, Anita had developed some interesting fascination about herself and the world around her mind. Focused on her studies, she was nothing less than Alice in the wonderland. Doing things strangely or doing strange things ... everything was normal for her. The family knew that she loved her family but she had a strange and mystic love for herself and her dreams.

Her family traditions didn't allow her to wear pair of jeans but her desires didn't pay heed. Her family wouldn't like her to sing loudly but she insisted and pushed her father to buy a radio for her.

Her father loved her strong opinions but was caged by his own code for the family. Anita was tall, had long hair and her eyes had deep intensity.

Whenever she would go to work, she would wear the pair of jeans underneath the salwar; She wouldn't take off the salwar after reaching but instead keep them on. There was a strange rush she got from this. The ability to keep something secret from others and to do it only to please yourself while letting the world believe otherwise, this was just one of such things that she was building.

A girl who wanted it first, used to run and pick the newspaper first, run towards the washroom and read it so that she would be the first one to know what happened in the world. She felt it was her right to know first and do things first.

Once her mother was serving food when she noticed Anita standing in front of the mirror and talking to her image "Hey Anita... You have become such a good-looking woman. Look at your dress; How fair and beautiful you look. All would be jealous!" ...

Her mother couldn't stop laughing and held her from behind. "So my little girl thinks that she has become smarter. Looks like I should get a boy for you to marry!!" she teased her. "Maa... Don't tease me. I will not marry so soon. I want to learn dancing or singing!" Anita interrupted.

"Well you can dance to the tunes of your dad for now... He is calling you and before he decides to find a guy for you, go and find a chair for yourself and sit there. I am getting your plate." Her mother taught her the reality.

"I will not marry until I learn singing... But what if my dad asks me to marry, what will I do? I can't say no to him. I am sure he is not going to get his 15 years old daughter married. I will get Anamika (her elder sister) married." She felt the stress and snapped out.

The moment her mother served her food, her father asked Anita "You should learn how to cook like Anamika. No family will like a daughter in law who doesn't know cooking."

"Dad, If I have to cook anyways when I get married, let me have some rest now. Besides, you promised me that I will learn singing. Anamika can learn cooking for she is elder and should be ready to cook." Anita said in low voice.

"Your mother in law will be very unhappy if you don't know how to cook." Her dad retorted.

"Or she might like it for I wont make food like you want but how she wants so I will learn from her and she will be happy too." She giggled and responded. Her father couldn't hold his smile and tried hitting her in love. She hugged him tightly and whispered "Don't get me married to any random guy. I don't like cooking."

Her father loved her for her wit and innocence. The whole family was very fond of Anita. She wasn't an easy child and sibling, but she was the life. Anamika was very domestic in her thoughts and Payal was quiet and aloof. Her brother Sunil loved her sisters and always felt he had the responsibility to take care of her sisters but never took anything seriously.

It was the morning of annual day at school and Anita had promised her friends that she will not wear a salwar and come in her pair of jeans. Anita's heart was beating for she would defy her father if she had done that but she was grandstanding in her thoughts.

Her father had asked her to eat her breakfast before she leaves; She wanted to take permission from her father to wear the pair of jeans. She walked towards her father and asked "Dad Can I ask for something?"

"What do you want? I haven't received the track of the money you spent last week? Don't ask for more money!" He responded.

"Dad I had promised my friends that ..." She continued.

"Who told you to promise?? What have you promised? He responded.

She took a deep breath and said "We will go to a temple close by after the school."

Her heart broke when she said that for, she felt something dying within her. She knew if she would have asked, her dad may have allowed but the fear of being judged by people around, her family and being looked as rebellious ... she dropped the idea. She walked into the room with her father's permission for something she didn't desire to. But she was sad that she couldn't even ask or say it. She walked towards her room, slowly and sad, removed her dupatta and lied on the bed, the tears trickled ... not for the fear of her father and the world but with her disappointment with herself...for not having the courage to say and do what she wanted to.

She lied lifeless for she lost the battle with herself once again... It wasn't the first time, and neither was going to be the last. A little girl who desired to dream yet not ready to fly for being judged ... for her guts and grit.

She didn't go to the annual party and slept over...

Noisy Wedding Bells

Anita was 19 years old now.... who had just joined the college and still used to wear jeans underneath the salwar. However, she had made one change; she had begun changing them in the college's washroom for few minutes. She wanted to admire herself in the mirror and the salwar again.

It was a beautiful breezy day and she was leaving for the college when she saw Dev standing with Payal. She looked at her sister and smirked; Payal was standing very close to Dev and blushing while Dev was playing with her hair and dupatta. Anita grinned for she had found another reason to blackmail her sister.

Dev liked Payal and used to follow her every day. Anita knew something was brewing between the two of them.

Both of them were standing at the corner of the street under the electricity pole early morning. Anita took a deep breath and ran towards her sister and screamed "Lets run!!!"; She held her hand and ran like a wind. Payal didn't know what had just happened and kept running after Anita. Everybody was staring at them running but Anita cared less and Payal was only concerned about her dupatta that was falling again and again. Payal was 'ashamed' of being caught by Anita and knew that Anita won't leave the chance.

"Why are you running like your thoughts?? Run fast Payal, we are getting late. If I do get late, I will tell dad about Dev and you." Anita kept talking while running and Payal was reassured of Anita harping onto Dev and her.

As soon as she reached the college, she stopped for a moment, was breathing heavily and left Payal's hand, walked towards the gate and said, "I will see you later" and smirked. She ran towards the class.

Payal stood stunned and confused for she was clueless... "Why did Anita take me along and why did I follow for my class doesn't start until next 1 hour?" Payal kept thinking and sat on the bench near the entry.

After the college got over, Payal walked towards Anita, pulled her with her hand and asked, "What happened earlier in the day?" Anita responded, "Nothing happened and that is a problem". They began walking towards the home. Payal didn't see Dev where she would usually see him while returning.

Dev was son of a family friend and wanted to help her father in some business project, so he used to visit regularly. Her father really liked Dev and Dev used to leverage this opportunity to see Payal but that day he was very scared for he knew Anita well and was suspecting that she would tell her parents.

To everyone's surprise, Anita was strangely quiet about all of it and didn't appear threatening.

Dev came to her place next day to meet her father for the project. Payal saw him entering and quietly moved to the kitchen.

While she was going to the kitchen, she heard her father talking to Dev to help him in searching for a suitable match for Anita as she was stepping into marriageable age.

Payal came running to tell Anita. "Dad wants to get you married now. Isn't he tired with Anamika's wedding already?" she screamed.

Anita was shocked and confused .... She couldn't have imagined that her dad would talk about her wedding so soon for her elder sister had got married recently and her elder brother was engaged already. She stood up in anger to shout at her father, but she saw herself in the mirror and the idea of wearing the wedding dress suddenly appeared a new fascination for she just felt something new was going to happen in her life. She went to the washroom and looked at herself in the mirror. She lifted her dupatta and put it on her head to see appear bride-like. Everybody thought she is depressed and crying inside but Alice was building a new wonderland in her mind.

Anita had made peace with the fact that she would never be able to build on her interest in singing for she knew she would chicken out. She knew she had to make peace with the fate. The fascination to have a man, to whom she could call her husband, was the new adrenaline rush for her.

She decided not to tease Payal anymore for she didn't want to upset Dev who was tasked to find a suitable guy for her. Instead she began teasing Payal for she was helping Payal to set the ground for her marriage and that Dev would do this job diligently with great interest.

Many young eligible men came to meet Anita, but she wasn't ready to meet; She told her mother that she wasn't sure about what to expect in the meeting or what could be the questions. Dev was sitting there listening to their conversations and he interrupted "If you want I can help you understand what may happen and that what would a man think."

"Sure... I am sure you would do this gladly." She looked at Payal and responded.

That night, the clan had prayer meeting for Shivratri. The whole clan was present and celebrating the auspicious day. The streets were lit up and the music was very enchanting.

While everyone was sitting, Dev's parents were talking to her parents about the usual stuff when Anita walked towards her parents to inform that Anamika had arrived. Dev parents looked at Anita and asked her mother if they are looking for a match for Anita. Her mother confirmed and mentioned that they wanted to start the discussions for a suitable boy and had asked Dev to help. Dev parents questioned if they would be interested in Dev and Anita's match. "Hmmmm we never thought of that. I think we can explore ... Let me speak to her father and come back. I think it will be great." Dev was known to be a Casanova for some and the family needed a nice simple girl.

Her mother discussed it with her father and they both were calibrated and called his parents for discussion. Dev and his parents came to her house; Dev was excited for he could see Payal and agreed to come along.

Both the parents were sitting in the room and discussed the idea. His parents called Dev and meanwhile Anita's parents took her to another room to discuss the alliance.

"We spoke to Dev's parents and we feel that both of you will be a good match. We have decided to marry both of you. Do you have any problem?" Her parents asked her and looked at her for a response. Anita couldn't believe what she heard. "DEV??!!! My husband?? ….." And there was silence in her mind. She couldn't have shared the Payal connection and couldn't have said no for they would have not considered him for Payal either … And anyways she didn't really have a choice. Her parents had decided and wanted her to set herself up for it.

She responded "I don't know anything… You both decide. Do ask Dev what he feels." Hoping that he might ask for Payal instead.

Her parents asked his parents about Dev's response. Dev had said yes too.

Anita's mother ran to get Anita dressed and they got the Roka ceremony done immediately.

Anita and Dev were sitting next to each other with their eyes looking down. Everybody thought that they were shy but only they knew what was happening within. Both the families hugged and they both sought their blessings by touching the feet of elders.

Everything looked orchestrated for the chain of events were unbelievable. Suddenly Deepak was quiet and Anita couldn't look into his eyes and didn't want to even try and see where Payal was.

Payal stood there celebrating her sister's engagement and stunned for she was at loss of words.

The ceremony got over and everyone returned to their rooms.

Anita looked at Payal with clueless eyes; Payal knew that Anita was helpless and she made peace with the reality. She couldn't manifest the emotions for letting go off the guy for all of this was new to her and wasn't a deep affair. She hugged Anita ... Anita held her tightly... They didn't speak a word.. There were no tears ... Only both of them knew what had transpired and only they could have understood the emotions... They held each other for 10 minutes. Payal pulled her back and told her "You know I love you and nothing can change that. You are my sister and I can't imagine you leaving us. I think now you should learn to cook and finally I will have the room for myself..." and laughed over it. Anita felt at ease and she hugged Payal again. Her mother came running and hugged both.

Anita entered her room and locked it. She looked at herself in the mirror and smiled. "I am going to marry a guy who was desired by every girl. Even Payal wanted to be with him but finally who gets the guy... Anita!!!" She was happy over the thought and began blushing.

The next day, his parents called her parents and asked about the date for official engagement ceremony. Her parents told them that they would consult the priest and confirm.

2 days later, it was decided that the Sunday of the following week would be auspicious for the engagement.

23rd Oct was the final date. All the invites were sent, and the bookings were done quickly. Fortunately, everything was falling in place. Sunil was excited for her little sister's engagement and worked to ensure that everything was perfect. He led the charge and her father didn't have to worry.

The D Day had arrived, and all the guests were there. Anita was wearing a pink suit embroidered with shinning stones. She was looking mesmerizing with the diamond necklace. Everybody couldn't get their eyes off her. Anita was excited to be at the center of everyone's attention. Dev was wearing traditional white shirt and pants.

The ceremony started and they both exchanged rings amidst the noise. They both looked at each other and smiled for this was the first day after the roka ceremony. The priest recited mantras and blessed the couple.

As a ritual, the parents asked the priest to suggest a date for the wedding basis the astrology.

After deep analysis, the priest said "Today!!! You wouldn't get a better day than today. Or next year" Everybody laughed and asked him to be serious. "I am not kidding. I think you should get them married today." He insisted.

Both the parents were confused with the weird suggestion and decided to discuss it with their families and return.

Anita and Dev were sitting on the stage along with the priest and both the families began delibrating. Anita's family was not ready for the wedding to happen the same day but Dev's parents saw merit in the priest's recommendation.

Both the parents moved towards the corner to discuss and finalize.

"Today won't be able possible at all. There is so much to do … And we can't get her married like that. We are not even prepared mentally and financially." Anita's parents insisted.

"What is important for us? Our kids are happy and have the blessings of god. We don't need anything and besides we have everyone here, so it saves you the money. What's the difference if it happens now or later? They will get married anyways so why let go off auspicious time. Let's do it. We will take our daughter in law home today!!" His parents insisted.

Anita's parents moved to her relatives and it was decided that the wedding would happen the same day. Anita's mother wedding dress was asked to be delivered at the venue from home; Her mother removed her necklaces, had Anita wear them along with her mother's bangles and both were dressed up for the moment in 3 hours. The wedding rituals began and both got married in 2 hours.

Everyone couldn't believe what happened in 5 hours. Anita and Deepak didn't have the time and mind space to realize that the life was changing. And it did.

Anita just moved into a new house!!!

Dev's mother was very happy to welcome her daughter in law and the whole clan was ready to welcome the eldest and the first daughter in law of the new generation.

Dev looked happy for he had made peace with Anita as her wife. A day prior, he had met Payal secretly to convince her for running away and getting married with him but Payal knew that this was beyond both of them and that she wouldn't sacrifice the prestige of the family and most importantly jeopardize her sister. She knew what was at stake and asked Dev to respect his responsibility towards his family and Anita..

Anita was taken into their room which was decorated. She didn't know what to expect and Dev was still clueless about how to take life forward.

While he was entering the room, his brother Sagar shouted "Why the hell are you getting a separate room?? What are you going to do anyways…? Just sleep!! What will you do with a wife whose has a mark on her eyebrows!! Can she even see??" His mother slapped Sagar; Anita could hear him, and she had a tear trickle down from her eyes. The 12-year-old Sagar had drawn a new red line and 19-year-old Anita knew that this is just the beginning and she was scared.

Building up the Storm

It was 8:00am in the morning and Anita was up for the morning prayers. Sagar was standing at the stairs when he saw Anita passing by.

"You should have been up by 7:00am but I guess you couldn't see the time." Sagar was at it again. Sagar was filled with anger and frustration after his cousin Gavin took him to a corner on the wedding night and told him that the first born would get the property rights and that Anita will take over from his mother as the one who decides the course of family.

He was filled with the anger, animosity, jealousy and arrogance of being the younger one. Anita knew that she need not focus on Sagar's provocative statements for he is young and nobody would understand.

Anita and Dev had formed a strong bond over their love for classical songs and music. Dev made peace with the fact that Anita is the woman who will take care of her family the best.

It was 31st Dec and Dev's mother had bought gold bangles for Anita as a gift for her birthday the next day. Sagar took his mother in a separate room and yelled "You want to give away everything to her …. She is going to take control and not let you survive … You are spending so much on her … What about me? Do you have anything left for me?". His mother was clueless about where these evil statements were coming from but her motherhood forced her to understand the 'pain' of her younger son.

Anita could hear everything, and she went to her mother in law's room and returned the bangles. "Maa, here you go. I don't need them." Anita said.

"Don't bother about what Sagar says, he is mad ... He is young. He doesn't know how to behave? Don't be upset!" She told Anita.

Anita denied and went back to her room. She sat on the chair... close to bed and cried ...for she couldn't figure Sagar's hatred. Dev saw her crying but decided to give her space and left from the room. Anita felt caged; worst than she did at her paternal house.

Anita thought that the true sense of being married is being lonely in the midst of strangers. The girl who had dreams to learn singing dancing and becoming something and now was crying for what she thought the new normal.

It was 1am when Dev entered the room and asked Anita if she is ok. "It doesn't matter. You should sleep. You have nothing to do in this." Anita tried avoiding any conversation for she knew that Dev wouldn't dare ask anything to his brother and mother.

The next day Dev asked his mother about the events that led to Anita crying whole day. His mother talked about Sagar's ill-intended words and his unusual behavior.

Dev couldn't believe but didn't know what to do. He told his mother "I think Sagar needs to be tamed for he can't disrespect anyone in the family and Anita is part of the family. "

He called Sagar and asked him for his actions and words. "Ever since she has come, nobody is focusing on me and the fact that we are spending money to make her feel nice relentlessly and I see nothing being saved for me and Monika. You are married now but what about us? I am still studying and need to get married. And Brother, if you believe me, I don't think she is right for you. She is not even good looking enough and doesn't deserve getting expensive jewelries but rather we should be spending money on business. She has a spell on you, and I see you loosing yourself in the process. She doesn't need to be treated nicely." Sagar just kept talking when Dev interrupted "I think let's stop discussing this... Mom, you need to fix what Sagar is saying". And Dev walked out.

His mother was helpless for she didn't want to lose her kids and knew that Anita had nothing to do with Sagar's behavior. She walked out .... Sagar stood in the room, smiling and feeling victorious for he knew he had stirred the focus from her to him.

New Dimensions New Lives

It was October when Anita realized that she was pregnant. Everyone was very happy and the whole house was excited to welcome new member except Sagar.... He wouldn't remain the youngest anymore and the additional partner of the property (which didn't exist) would be born.

His mother was very happy and told everyone. Watching his mother talking to relatives, he screamed "We can't even support food for 5 of us and he is thinking of making babies .... stressing us all out. He will have more kids and then kick all of us out. You need to stop or else I will run away." He walked out of the room... leaving his mother stunned but she couldn't stop thinking about her grandchild.

After speaking to her relatives, she decided to speak to Sagar. She went to his room and saw that he was sitting in anger on the bed. His mother knew that her son was losing himself and was feeling insecure. She decided to ask Dev and Sagar to begin working together and that Dev should give 30% of the earning to Sagar so that he felt better.

"But Maa, he doesn't even have a family of his own and giving him 30% of our earnings will make him go mindless more than he is already. You should pay attention to really what he utters, and his nonstop bashing of Anita is not good for her health in this stage. Can you put some sense into him instead of trying to fan his mind?" Dev couldn't hold back and left. His mother felt torned apart between 2 sons. She knew Dev was right but was aware of Sagar's insecurities.

Dev conceded to his mother's suggestions and Sagar saw this as the first victory and realized that he was winning with his designs.

Months passed and his mother made conscious effort to ensure that Anita gets the much needed space and care. August 5 and it was time for her delivery …. The doctor told the family that she needed to be hospitalized for the delivery, for there were complications.

Sagar had a smirk on his face for he expected the worst to happen. The family got her admitted immediately for the delivery; She had to stay in the hospital for hours and the doctors couldn't get the baby out.

Dev came inside the operation theatre and held Anita's hand. She was in deep pain and didn't want Dev to leave and requested the doctor for him to stay in. Thinking it might help, the doctors agreed. Several hours had passed and they couldn't get the baby out until early morning when they finally managed to get the baby out. IT WAS A GIRL!!!

The whole family was on top of the moon. The first grandchild of the family was born, and it was a girl. His mother was very happy and couldn't stop gushing over her granddaughter.

Sagar was very unhappy. He thought that the whole savings will now be directed to marry her, and he will have nothing for him, his wife and kids.

He dragged his mother away from the celebrations and told her that she needs to fix this injustice to him and his future family.

Dev's mother couldn't believe what she was listening "Can you stop this Sagar? This is the moment to celebrate. Everything will be ok. You don't worry. Your mom is here. I promise I will never let you suffer." Dev's mother promised …. something which turned out fatal for herself in the future.

Ria became the eye of the apple for everyone. Both the grandparents adored Ria and took good care of her. Her childhood became a reason for the family to relive and spread happiness. Anita's life began revolving around her and Dev formed a very strong bond with her daughter.

Anita knew that she would always stand up for her kids and sacrifice everything to keep them happy and not let them suffer like she did.

Years passed. Sagar didn't stop but Anita didn't give much importance to him and his ill intended actions. She maintained distance from Sagar and everyone in the family knew of the unsaid silence between the two.

It was one of the Sunday evening and Sagar walked towards Anita's room to inspect the room. His niece was sitting in the room and ran towards him. She felt chocolate in his pocket and asked for the chocolate. He pushed her away and shouted "So now you wouldn't even let me have my chocolate. Did your mother teach you to grab everything? Go ask your father for food; He loves producing kids right!! He should be thinking of feeding as well, I am sure. Not my share anymore."

"Sagar!!! Have some shame ... You are her uncle... Watch what you are doing... Watch your words... She is an innocent child. What harm has she done to you? I have listened to all the crap you have said all my life to me ... But not my kids... Enough is enough.!!!" Sagar couldn't believe that Anita shouted and confronted him.

"Ohh so this is real you... You will now shout at me. Who gave you the right??? You should know that you are lucky that my brother sticked around with you ... you can't even see and he is putting up with you... You have put a spell on him and the whole family. You want to grab everything and now you have picked up the route of using kids." Saimond shouted. His mother entered the room and interrupted "What the hell is going on?"

"Ma, you should hear what he is saying, and this is enough of him.... He is not too old to shout and treat me like this. She is a small child and he is jealous of her. I can't even believe he can be so evil and inhuman." Anita blasted and couldn't stop.

"Anita, hold yourself. Look what you are saying." His mother interrupted.

"Ma, if you don't stop him now, he will never listen to you, look at his age and listen to his thoughts in his mind and the words he uses. This isn't the first time... He didn't even spare his brother... leave me aside. You really need to do something.. for an 18-year-old couldn't be thinking like this." Anita responded and walked out.

Anita narrated everything to Dev. He looked at her face; Anita was fuming this time and not crying and he knew that the things are not the same anymore.

Dev told his mother that this couldn't go on more and that he thinks that the house needs to be divided and she can take care of Sagar; While he will continue to support the family, but he cant have Sagar interfere in any capacity in the family.

Dev's mother looked at him and couldn't believe that Dev asked for separation. The same son who loved his mother more than anything was contemplating separation. She knew this wasn't healthy, but things were not in control and it was decided that the ground floor will be given to Dev and Sagar and the parents will stay on the first floor.

Sagar was delighted with what had happened and his mother saw him smiling; helpless and wrapped in the sheets of her son's love.

Not the same Anymore

This was her 10th year of married life; 2 daughters 1 son. Anita and Dev had left the house few years later for Sagar began bullying and messing up the ambience in the house.

Sagar began cheating people and his brother and Dev had made up his mind that he wouldn't want his kids to experience any of it. His mother was blindly in love for Sagar. He tricked women to fall for him and then dumped them. His marriage didn't last more than 3 months for he couldn't conceive …. Life was coming full circle for him.

But Anita was far away from all this. She had moved out in a rented apartment with her husband and Kids and life was tough yet normal. The kids were growing and needed her attention. She had found a new life; she created her social network of influential women and had an active social life.

Weeks after the anniversary celebration, the tragedy hit the family.

Early morning Anita got a call from her father in law informing that her mother in law passed away. She felt choked… Anita had always admired, respected her mother in law despite her actions. She began crying, pulled Dev from the bed and hugged him. Dev couldn't believe the news. His heart was beating, eyes popped out and held Anita tightly. Anita informed the kids and everyone began crying.

While the kids had stayed away, they had strong bond with their grandmother. Her son had loved her grandmother more than Anita and things just came full circle.

Anita had formed a special place in her mother in law's heart as the best daughter-in-law anyone could get, and all the relatives echoed her. The whole clan was looking up to Anita to give a deserving farewell to her mother in law.

She reached Sagar's house and hugged her father in law. She moved towards her mother-in-law's body; held her in her hands, caressed her face and hugged. The tears began trickling and she knew she was going to miss a very strong relationship. Everyone was stunned and shocked. Sagar had made peace with the fact that Anita deserved more than what she got, and he touched her feet and hugged her to seek assurance. Anita took charge of the whole rituals and ensured that no stone was left unturned to give her befitting farewell. It was a grandeur affair and the whole clan was shocked with the love, care, respect and traditions, the family bid farewell to Dev's mother.

Though everyone knew that she will do her best, Anita knew the stature of her mother in law and didn't want to underplay the journey of a strong woman. The whole clan followed her and her mother in law was laid to rest with proper rituals.

Sagar's behavior change was temporary, and Anita/Dev knew that already so when he asked to settle things up, Anita opted out and said that it would be in the best interest of the family that they continue to stay away like they have.

Anita knew that her mother in law was the last thread between Sagar and Anita and with her death, it didn't exist anymore. Dev's father continued to remain on self-imposed exile with Sagar and didn't want to live with anyone else, so Anita and Dev didn't pursue him. A very important bond was coming to an end and Anita knew it was inevitable.

The Storm that She Didn't Deserve

Anita was now a grandmother. She was a content grandmother; Her son chose to remain unmarried and she began to realize the importance of living for herself and spending time with her husband. Dev was going through a rough patch of years of no work and being financially dependent on his son. This was too heavy on his manhood and man ego. He felt no sense of purpose and began losing his mind in the process. He had started fighting with her to exhale the negativity that he was building within.

It was a sunny afternoon and Anita was busy with her daily chores. While She was cleaning the kitchen, she heard Dev talking and smiling with someone and blushing. She was noticing a very unusual behavior and it was building up within, but she didn't pursue it actively.

Dev had hired a girl, his daughter age, as an employee in his shop. Spending most of the time with her he began forming an intimate relationship and strangely she began visiting their home frequently. Anita was suspicious of all of this but never gave a serious thought until that day.

One day while she was watching TV, Dev was video chatting using ear phones.

Anita decided to mute the TV and hear the conversation. Dev was flirting with a woman and was using explicit language. Anita was shocked and felt unarmed and numb.

She didn't know what to do and react. Whom to talk to for it could spoil Dev's image. What may have been a joke for her earlier was killing her within. She didn't say anything and remained quiet. Dev didn't realize. Anita walked out towards the kitchen for she couldn't believe and didn't want to lose her cool.

Aftre sometime, Dev went to the kitchen. When Anita saw him entering the kitchen, she threw the bowl of chopped veggies, held in her hand, on the floor.

Dev questioned the act and Anita couldn't control and slapped Dev.

"Ask your conscience if it at all it exists, what have you been doing!!! You should be ashamed of yourself for having an affair with a woman of your daughter's age. 30 years of marriage and sacrifice for you and your family to earn this cheat. You have flushed the only thing you had manage to earn … your respect and that bitch couldn't find anyone but a father's age man who is also a grandfather."

She added "You have left me with no space and didn't care about how kids and your grandkids will feel. How would the world look at you if her parents decide to storm into our colony and shamed you? Do you have no shame and respect left? What did I do to earn this in my life? All my life I lived with you when your family insulted me, and now that the family isn't there, you have taken the charge to disrespect me and my existence. Do you realize how depressed I have been with these thoughts for so many months…? I was trying to evade but the filth you have been talking couldn't store up more than this. Where will you hide yourself now? What do you think your kids will think and feel? You have messed up our hard-earned respect and love with your insanity and nothing less than vulgarity…." And Anita couldn't stop crying for she couldn't believe she used such language for Dev.

Dev had nowhere to hide. There was absolute silence in the house for days; Anita felt suffocated but was scared to tell her daughters or son until one day she couldn't hold and told her elder daughter.

Her daughter was speechless and didn't know how to manage this. She called her brother to tell him about the father. The son was fuming and couldn't stop crying for crushing his mother's feelings who he loved dearly.

He recommended to abandon Dev and have him realize his deeds. There was a deep sense of sorrow in the family. Anita's son wasn't ready to concede his father fault, but his partner forced his to think about his father's situation and that the matter was between a husband and wife.

Her kids told her that she needed to decide the next action. Anita had nothing to decide. She had nothing to choose from and felt crippled. She couldn't imagine and couldn't tell anyone how stunned she was

Anita decided to visit her son along with her daughters without anyone else. She spent great time with the kids. She went out for a movie after a long time and dinned out.

Dev had become her strength through these years and his actions hammered her the worst.

She didn't talk to Dev for weeks until one day Dev asked her to give him a chance to explain. Dev explained the reasons and things that led him. Anita was in no mood and had realized that nothing is permanent.

The incident opened all the shackles of her life that she had since childhood and decided to do everything she deserved and wanted.

She learned how to use Facebook, built her own profile and began writing poems and romantic couplets to impress herself and enjoy life.

She invested in building her social profile and writing books. She had a deep sense of freedom and realized that as much as Dev loved her and that he deserved a chance for being with her through thick and thins, she had also realized the importance of taking care of herself and desires.

She knew she needed to focus on her dreams that she had since childhood; To Sing. She began recording videos for her own YouTube Channel. Just 48 hours of launching, she had had hit 900+ requests.... She opened her phone to see people texting on her videos "Cute :')", "Hawttttie." Cute girl", "What a voice?". She knew she had arrived!!!

"LIVING YOUR LIFE THE WAY YOU WANT IT MAKES YOU NOT HAVE ANY REGRETS... DON'T LET GO OFF THE CHOICE TO CHOOSE."

"ITS GONNA BE OK AND IN DARK ROOMS LIES THE POWER OF LIGHTS... UPS AND DOWNS TELLS WHO YOU ARE"

Another Life Another Day

Staying in the four walls of the house, Rhea was super excited of her turning 16. The guys at the school used to check her out every day for she used to lift her knee length skirts to look cool. The whole girl gang was famous for the show. Rhea was the talk of every boy's table and her seniors checked her gang out everyday, but she had crush over her junior who had grey eyes.

She couldn't resist the rough and tough look guy and knew that it was insane to date a younger boy but the thought of it made her super excited. Richie began stalking her outside school and even her house.

He began stalking her around 5:00pm everyday and was almost noticed by the neighbors. Rhea used to stand on the terrace like a princess for the subjects to see and used to melt like a candle when Richie passed by the roads.

This went on for long until Richie decided to move to different city for studies. Rhea had no clue about his whereabouts. She felt miserable yet began searching for a new crush.

Rhea was tall enough, long hair and fair ... Deep eyes and a cute yet insane smile.

It was his uncle's wedding when Kartik had travelled from Mumbai to Delhi. Kartik was a cute looking guy who was little heavier. Rhea didn't notice Kartik until the family prayers function. And then she began noticing that Kartik was constantly looking at her throughout. Kartik was mesmerized by Rhea and was hopelessly attracted to her. He couldn't resist and began flirting with her.

Rhea didn't realize but she began enjoying the attention without conceding the truth. She began responding to Kartik's passes subtly and had formed fascination for him.

It was pre-cocktail night, and everybody was tired; sleeping like frogs all over in the house. Kartik and Rhea were sleeping close on the floor. Kartik opened his eyes and looked around to see who was sleeping. He moved a little towards Rhea and after establishing that no one was up, he quickly looked into her eyes and kissed her. Rhea couldn't hold and slapped him. Nobody heard the sound and she pushed him away.

Rhea didn't like the uninvited kiss and Kartik being too 'fast' with things. She decided to teach Kartik a lesson and stopped talking or acknowledging his presence. But it didn't deter Kartik to chase her.

Few days later, he sent her an apology letter, seeking for her attention back. Rhea knew that Kartik was genuine but thought that Kartik was too Casanova kind and that she wouldn't want to waste her time.

But his consistent persistence and Rhea's fascination of attention broke the ice and they began flirting around during ceremonial events. Rhea knew nothing was serious and just wanted to enjoy the attention.

It was the day after reception when Kartik whispered to Rhea that the family is contemplating getting us married and that he cannot come out and claim that both were already setting up things. Rhea laughed over it and was excited with the idea of setting up an arrange marriage.

While Kartik was a nice guy but his weight was one reason Rhea was not sure if she would want to marry.

Finally, the proposal came to her parents officially and they asked Rhea for her answer. She told her mother about her apprehensions and appeared clueless on how to deal with this situation.

She didn't want to hurt anyone but didn't know what she should do. Her aunt persuaded her that she should focus on the guy's background and character along with financial status than weight and all.

She argued that they both won't look nice together which was rubbished by her aunt with the reason that men look nice when heavy and that he is good looking and fair too and that we don't get everything in our lives and if most of the boxes are met, it should be a deserving yes.

Rhea didn't know how to manage and what to do. She relied on the best judgement of her family and said yes. She was, though, excited about being married and the whole process of Roka and family celebrating.

This was her first official event for which she went to a salon.

She was excited and the whole family was looking forward to the event. The family celebrated the union and blessed the couple.

They both exchanged the rings and decided to talk about the wedding dates as well. Kartik stood and told everyone that he was not financially stable back in Mumbai and needs time to marry so that he could have a better house and settled job to marry.

Rhea's parents appreciated Kartik's decision and decided to respect his emotions. Rhea was happy that this gave her time to study and go to college and finish her graduation. She was happy and felt nice that Kartik was taking things seriously and she knew her decision was right and felt at ease.

Kartik flew back to Mumbai with his mother and Rhea was excited about the possibilities coming up.

Months later, her father had a bad business downfall and had to move back to their old house. Rhea couldn't adjust but didn't have a choice.

She couldn't resist and began visiting a computer café to chat with men in chat room. She was thrilled with the process. Vihaan used to visit the café and saw Rhea sitting and laughing out loud. Vihaan was blown away with Rhea and began to follow her for few days to realize that she stayed in the same colony.

Rhea began noticing this and enjoyed the attention. The first time she saw Vihaan clearly, she felt very different. The old house was small one and Rhea used to come to balcony and look at Vihaan staring at her.

Her father got her to study computers by Vihaan's brother. Rhea was super excited for she felt some deep connection. She began using this as a reason to meet Vihaan and they both began spending extra time to 'study'.

They spoke for hours and hours and felt deep connection. They kept talking and desired to talk more. Everyday they began skipping their colleges to meet outside a temple and roam around on the bike for long hours.

Not an iota of kissing or anything except holding eachother. Vihaan was obsessed and deeply in love with Rhea and Rhea felt special with him around.

She didn't know the reason for such connection but began looking for times to meet. He used to jump through the terraces to meet Rhea on her terrace and even had to run away soon for her uncle used to come up for smoking.

It was Holi when Rhea called Vihaan over her terrace. Everybody had gone back to their homes to dry up and Vihaan jumped through 4 houses between theirs. Rhea had an under-construction room area on the terrace where she dragged Vihaan in. The moment Vihaan entered, she kissed him passionately and they kissed for long until he kissed her neck and Rhea moaned loudly.

This was first time when Rhea and Vihaan had sex. They went on for 3 hours on stones kept and madly looked into eachother's eye. That day Rhea felt different, and she felt heavenly. She couldn't stop gushing over the feeling.

She went down for dinner when her mother gave her the letter from Kartik. Rhea was clueless. Reality had hit her suddenly. Everything seemed shattering in front of her eyes and she read the first letter by Kartik stating how much he misses her and that he was striving hard for their future as husband and wife.

And the letter had cassettes of romantic songs for her. Every week she began receiving letters from Kartik and eachtime it reminded Rhea of the reality, but she couldn't stop and resist Vihaan for it felt beyond intimacy, but soul connect.

She began responding to the letters as a respect to the man and sending him gifts to build up his illusion of her love. She hid her true feelings and wrote things for Kartik to avoid any confrontation.

The fire of Rhea and Vihaan began spreading smoke around and her mother realized it. She called her and told her to fix it before she did anything about it. Rhea had no clue what to do and how to manage and if she should even manage and let things go on.

Vihaan began insisting that she should talk to her father and convince him of him. The conversations between them turned hostile and he pushed her to talk to her father. Rhea couldn't build the guts to talk to her father, but her father had gauged it already.

It was a dark moonless night when Vihaan's mother ran towards Rhea's house to complain and pushed her to stop seeing him. While she was suffering from cancer, she was worried for her son as Vihaan had threatened to kill himself.

Rhea was quiet when her phone rang; she ran to answer the phone.

Rhea: "Hello"

Vihaan: "I am going to eat sleeping pills and let train run over me if you don't tell your father or run away with me?"

Rhea: "What the hell are you talking about? Don't make it difficult for me. I am not in the state to do what you want me to do?

Vihaan: "Then be ready to hear the news for me to die."

Rhea: "What are are talking? Can you please stop? Where are you? You have to swear that you are not going to do anything. If you love me and if you value me, you will not hurt yourself. Please don't do this."

Vihaan: "I can't live without you. I can't imagine myself without you. You are my life… How can you even imagine to be with someone else? You are only mine. How dare you push yourself to marry anyone else? You don't have the right over yourself. You are mine. Are you mad stupid … I love you and you know how much you matter to me."

Rhea: "Vihaan, please I beg you. I don't know right now what to do but I want you to just come home. If you don't come home in 1 hour and show me yourself at the window….."

(Everyday they used to see each other at the window of their balcony and used to talk without the words but through eyes.

They didn't fear even the neighbors seeing them and they had begun gossiping. Rhea's father was a well-known man in the colony. Vihaan would step out without the shirt and Rhea would look at her toned body and brown eyes.

They didn't have much intimacy, but this was about soul meeting soul… Soul talking to another soul… He would carry his sipper and kiss the sipper like he would want to kiss her. Rhea would move her hands around her neck like she would want him to touch. The window became their coffee table in the conversations and whenever they would be sitting there with family, they would still look at eachother and talk through their smiles.

Vihaan would offer her water, if she would cough, through eyes. Before going to sleep, Vihaan would want Rhea to come and show him her face and give a flying kiss; that's how his soul like he used to say would feel the kiss. Even when she couldn't come to the balcony, she would look through the entry gate and kiss from the small hole. And while these mad people where deeply diving into the love, someone was noticing this.

Violin knew what was happening and he suspected that there was something that Rhea was upto … and that it wasn't right for her to do this considering she was engaged.

Violin began forming more love and respect for his would-be brother in law and began tracking her actions and movement.)

Rhea disconnected the phone. While she did, her heart was beating fast for she didn't know what he might do and that she forgot to ask where he was.

And then regretted that she shouldn't have been angry with him. What if he had become angrier and did something stupid.

She couldn't hold herself and she ran to her dad and begged him to save Vihaan and that she will do everything that her father wanted her in return of saving him.

Vihaan's mother was still there when she heard her. She began crying and ran towards her house. She couldn't breath properly.

Rhea was crying and couldn't breathe. She was lying on the bed and was crying for mercy and for his life to be saved. She told her father" Please save him please save him…. If anything happens to him, I will do something to myself and then you can get me married to Karthik. If something happens, I will not live even if you get me married to Kartik."

Rhea's mother slapped her and shouted "What the hell are you doing? What the hell are you pushing yourself and for a guy who doesn't even have a job and isn't extremely good looking".

Rhea screamed and shouted "Don't say anything to him; you will see the worst of me if you uttered anything negative for him. He is my soul and I love him the way he is. And don't think I am any princess that you are treating him like this. What has he done to you? He loves and respects you so much and wants to marry me. If he wanted to use me, he could have done a lot and abandoned me pregnant. Then you could have done nothing. Don't say anything wrong about him. I can't listen. He loves Violin for he thinks he is the only sane member of the family. He worries for Fiza and that she is a nice girl. What else do you want? If you think Vihaan doesn't have a job, what is Kartik upto? He is also not working or wasn't working when I got engaged."

"Our families dont make relationships like a deal. You dated Richie... You didn't like him then you moved to someone else. Then you loved Kartik... we got you engaged to him... we didn't push you to marry him. We asked you if you wanted to. Relationships aren't like clothes that you keep changing. If you don't like what you liked earlier, you wanna change it. I asked you to say no if you didn't want to marry Kartik and we would have said no. You can't put your father through this. The whole family is involved. You are treating marriage like a game. Now you don't like Kartik and you wanna marry Vihaan. Society looks at such people as your friend Helly..." Her mother couldn't control and retorted.

" What are you saying... You are comparing me with Helly!!! How are you talking... as if I am a whore... Pls don't make me look like this? I can't take it. I am not saying anything. I will marry whosoever you want me to but please save him. If he dies, I wont survive either and then you can deal with all this yourself." Rhea interrupted.

(Helly was a very close friend of Rhea and used to take her along to a lot of trips until she realized that she was a sex worker and was intending to drag Rhea into it. Rhea was fair good-looking girl with wavy hair and eyes of a peacock and smile of a child. She looked fresh like sky and flowers and vibrant as a valley of roses. And Helly saw a strong partner in her business in form of Rhea until one day Rhea's dad figured out about her and almost saved Rhea from being honey trapped.)

"How selfish are you? You don't care about your father your mother your siblings? He is the only person who matters. If he makes you abandon your family, he isnt good for you anyways. What are you doing to your father who has only lived his life basis his reputation and how he has earned it? And now we have people coming our way telling us to take care of our daughter or else they would broadcast that she puts spell on boys towards her. Your father sacrificed so much for you .. for the family and you should be ashamed of pushing him in the gutter of shame." Her mother couldn't hold herself.

"If you think you can be happy with him putting us all through this shame and misery of life, don't be surprised that you may not remain happy with him. You can't be happy while burning so many lives and families for your selfish interests. Our families don't operate marriages like everyday business." Her mother continued.

"How can you curse your own daughter? You are doing this for a guy who is not even your blood. But you are cursing your own blood. What wrong has Vihaan done to you? Why such hatred? He respects you a lot." Rhea reacted.

" I don't care about Vihaan or Kartik but if something happens to your dad and I lose him and become widow, you are responsible and culprit of trading your father for Vihaan. And this won't stop at just him and many more will follow" Rhea's mother was almost fuming and was at her worst.

Kartik had no clue of what was transpiring behind. He was building a life of new dreams. To settle a new house for his wife.. his family and start a new family. Kartik had had a very tough childhood. His father had died a year ago and he had no clue about family planning. Kartik sold his house to buy a bigger house and began his business for now he was responsible for his entire family.

Kartik always felt alienated and unusual; He had so many secrets suppressed in his mind since childhood and he couldn't come to terms with his identity. And this was his chance to move on and start a new life with the woman he loved. The woman for whom he used to write letters for ... songs for her,... send her gifts and cassettes to express his feelings. He was always unsure if he will be enough for his future wife.

He was building a castle of a new life and new dreams without knowing that the castle was crumbling even before it could begin.

Rhea had figured out by that moment that her family wasn't going to bend and she insisted to save Vihaan. Rhea's father loved Rhea enough to go and get him safe back home.

Rhea knew that this was coming an end. She knew that she won't be able to marry Vihaan in this life and was ready to have the bitter pill in exchange to save Vihaan.

She realized that the stakes were higher than she thought.

Rhea's extended family was for no good use; they were wanting to milk the situation to embarrass her father and the personal ego was all out to burn his respect into ashes. Rhea knew of the reality and the fact that her extended family was making enough effort to create ripples.

Rhea's father came back home after ensuring Vihaan's safe return, but he realized that the time was ripe to leave the place and move in somewhere else before this could blow out more.

Rhea knew the reality and she decided to be with her father. The whole family moved away from the city to save the crumbling family. Vihaan didn't stop stalking her. He tracked her new house through her aunt, who was desperate to spoil the marriage and be entertained with the fire in her backyard.

Rhea knew about Vihaan's madness and that he would have followed her. He continued to follow and see her on terrace, but Rhea realized that she was not going to be able to live upto her promise. She asked Vihaan to promise her and not see her again. She was asking her soul to stay away from her body, but she knew that she would otherwise sacrifice Vihaan and her father.

The wedding date was nearing. 3 years of courtship was coming to logical conclusion and the whole family was ready to celebrate. Nobody knew what was happening and Rhea went ahead with all rituals.

It was the morning of 8th Dec for her wedding. It felt like the world is coming to halt. Everyone was immersed in the happiness of marrying the eldest daugther of the clan amongst her cousins. It was grand event and her father wanted to ensure that her wedding was a known and talked about.

He pulled all plugs and made it grand putting himself through steep debts. Rhea knew that the night was going to be difficult but she knew that she couldn't fight her fate and that while she couldn't change her feelings for Vihaan, it was important to let go off him for his safety.

Vihaan was hospitalized for he had eaten sleeping pills enough to kill him. Rhea didn't know what was happening for the rituals kepts her closed and disconnected to the other world.

The venue was lit up and all the attendees began coming. Rhea walked in and the whole world stood frozen. She looked like a fairy tale and it felt like like the god was there to celebrate her wedding.

Kartik's father was very fond of Rhea as the family knew eachother since childhood and both Kartik and Rhea had seen eachother as kids. And years before his death, his father had desired to marry Kartik and Rhea.

It was discredited for they were too young then, but his father always wanted Rhea to be Kartik's wife.; Maybe he had foreseen a strong woman in Rhea who could nurture his family/heirs and stand tall for his family as a strong woman.

Kartik's father knew of the vultures around to encroach and knew that he needed a strong sensitive and a girl of high emotions and ethics to take care of his family and Rhea would have proven exactly the same; Rhea's father was known as a man of principles and respect.

Kartik was looked as a big catch in the clan for he was single son and the family had reputation of being rich and high-class family. A lot of other relatives had desired to marry Kartik with their daughter and they didn't miss any opportunity to create ripples in the relationships, but somethings are truly written in heaven to happen.

Rhea walked in and everyone couldn't get off their eyes from her. She looked divine and was glowing as a heavenly blessing. She walked in with the innocence of a tender young girl who was ready to put all at back and make honest attempt to give this life a new chance.

The ceremonies began, and Ria was married to the Kartik. Rhea didn't know that Vihaan was hospitalized and that her aunt made her last attempt to create ripples by visiting him in the hospital to create and hear gossip.

Rhea had to move to Mumbai, and she knew that she was leaving a part of her life behind ... unsure and unaware of what life was going to bring to her.

Rhea began settling down in her married life and her childhood dream to be in Mumbai was fulfilled.

Kartik left no stone unturned to ensure that the family was happy though she went through troubled times with her mother in law. She eventually made peace with her and realized that this was the natual process for a mother. Years went by, Vihaan tried contacting Rhea and even seeing in Mumbai but couldn't succeed.

Meanwhile, Vihaan's mother was unwell and forced him to marry one of his friend. Rhea was settling in her married life and had 2 beautiful kids. She had made peace and began enjoying the life.

This Tsunami Didn't Knock At All

Violin had left his home. When he had just reached work, Kartik called Violin

Kartik: "Do you know Vihaan? I am sending you a photo.... see the photo and tell me if you know who this guy is."

Violin's heart began beating fast. He knew some storm is about to hit the family and he suddenly thought and prayed that its not Vihaan. 17 years had passed for this.

Violin opened his phone and the whole world was falling in front of his eyes. He knew that this storm might engulf the whole family and he caught cold feet. It was Vihaan's photo. Violin pretended unaware and responded in negative.

Kartik probed further and asked him to answer truthfully and made him swear god. Violin silently prayed to god to save the family to crumble in whatever way he can and that he was going to lie to save the family, kids and the future. Violin continued to pretend unsure.

Then Kartik responded by showing more photos which were intimate.

So, Rhea and Kartik were experiencing a low tide in their relationship for few months and Rhea had confided in Violin about their issues. Kartik began drinking and using explicits as a normal and Rhea complained of being treated as a sex object for her sexual desires were very low and Kartik was sexually very active.

Also, Violin had confessed that their father had orchestrated the drama of ill health during her wedding to push her to marry and she felt cheated and hurt. Violin didn't realize then that he was setting the stage for the storm to hit the family.

Kartik told Violin that Rhea had been traveling to places all by herself and was involved physically with Vihaan. And that she was talking to some one suspicious everyday for longer hours.

Violin controlled his emotions and probed further for what made him think. Rhea was pregnant, and both Kartik/Rhea wanted abortion done.

While she was hospitalized, Rhea had handed over her phone to Kartik. Kartik had suspected if Rhea had turned asexual or lesbian with her closeness to her girlfriends and suspected her no play on bed as an outcome of these issues.

Violin probed Kartik for where was he. Kartik responded that he had dropped Rhea at home and had come out or else he would have killed her. It was raining heavily, and he had parked his car away from the house on the road. Kartik asked Violin to come to Mumbai and save him or else he would lose himself. Violin was shaking and for he felt he was the culprit for this leading Rhea to imagine her life before marriage. Violin had too many thoughts running;

"I hope nothing happens to Kartik by the time I take the flight!"

"Where will I find Kartik?"

"What if he needs medical help for he had had 6 high energy drinks and there is no one around?"

"What will I tell family?"

What will happen if Kartik decides to abandon her and the kids?"

What will be Rhea's future?

What if Rhea does harm herself?

What would the relatives talk it as ?

What will he tell Anuj?

How will the work happen?

"Right now, Kartik's life is more important than anything else. Right now I need to put some sense in Kartik's head" Violin thought. But how could he, when he would act more aggressively had he been in the situation?"

Violin came out of those thoughts and asked Kartik "Did you ask Rhea about this?"

Kartik responded "Had I, I would have killed her or myself. I couldn't stand her, and I left."

Violin asked further "So what do you want to do?... What do you think led her to do this; You know she has been loyal to you and the family... You know she is emotional person and has been invested with you and kids and family way too much so why would such a person do something like this? Could this be just your imagination and that this was just one side of the story?"

Violin knew that this wasn't making sense for a man who had just realized that his wife could be cheating on him, but he had no other choice to control his emotions and kept his focus on saving their family and the kids.

Kartik mentioned that he didn't want to live with her and wanted a divorce and that he should also call her parents to settle this for he couldnt live with this.

Violin told Kartik about Rhea talking about her issues with him and that how she felt as a wife. Kartik agreed to Rhea's version of the story and added that he didn't know what he should be doing to fix this. He requested Violin to leave everything and come to Mumbai.

Violin was stunned. He didn't know how to save this from falling and crumbling. He closed his eyes and prayed god to save this from spreading like fire and save the family.

He told Kartik that he would take the flight immediately. He called Anuj to help him pack clothes so that he could go to the airport directly. He couldn't have told Anuj about everything for it was too overwhelming and didn't know what to tell and left stating that Rhea/Kartik were going through a rough patch.

Violin told his parents that Rhea's health had deterioted and that their tickets are booked to travel to Mumbai later in the evening. The parents were shocked and didn't know how to react. Violin knew that he had to prepare himself to hold the storm together before it killed everyone in the journey. He ran and flew to Mumbai. His flight was late and Kartik was waiting for him at the airport.

Rhea knew about Violin's visit but was not aware of the reason. Violin reached Mumbai and met Kartik. He was fine but was experiencing pain in the chest and Violin was worried. He took him to the hospital and the doctor told him to sleep for the energy drinks were playing.

Violin took Kartik home and made it appear to the kids and Rhea that everything was normal. His heart was beating. The kids needed to be dropped to school.

Violin dropped the kids to school but was scared that they may erupt in a war while he had stepped out to drop. He left it to the god and came back to realize that the inevitable had happened and Rhea had figured out the reason of his visit.

Violin took a deep breath; full of fear and worry to lose everything. Kartik began shouting and screaming crying for being cheated. His childhood secrets were out of the closet.

He argued with her and slapped her. And Rhea began crying for making it a public affair and that it needed to be sorted between the husband and wife without involving her family.

She felt humiliated and saw her image shattering everywhere.

When she learnt that her parents were coming too, she knew that this wasn't going to be cordial and was blown out of control. She began hurting herself. Violin held her and told her that it didn't make her a bad person and that he would support her irrespective even though he agreed with Kartik. Kartik realized that he may have missed the chance to fix things by involving others and Rhea began screaming and crying for she felt she didn't deserve this. Violin pushed both of them in different rooms for he had to get the kids back from school.

The kids came and Kartik/Rhea were lying lifeless on the bed. The kids had no clue but knew something major had happened. Violin's parents had reached and began complaining of what they had been put through after so many years and Rhea may have messed up her family and kids for good.

Violin knew that he needed to tame his parents and told them to remain quiet and not dramatize it; or not to alienate Rhea if they wanted to save her and Kartik alongwith their family.

Violin had lost track of time and dropped kids for their classes. When he returned, he saw his parents sitting in a room; commenting and talking to eachother with Rhea and Kartik sitting around ... stating that it could have been an evil eye and that they should hug eachother and sort this out.

Violin saw history repeating where the issues were being shelved under the carpet. He screamed at both of them and asked them to move out and that they needed to stop old tricks .... that it might not go unsettled in a snap and they needed to address the real issues and not make it look easy. His parents were fuming but knew that their son was right.

Violin dragged them out of the room to let Rhea and Kartik talk.

Violin was fuming but remain focused to keep the focus on both Kartik and Rhea. Rhea and Kartik spoke for hours in the room and decided to go out and talk freely.

Vihaan was stressed and kept arguing with his parents for trying old trciks and that they needed to be watchful.

Hours later, they returned and knew the sanity that they needed to maintain while sorting the real issues and look at the larger life.

Kartik called Violin in a separate room and told him that he would take it forward and would manage things. And that they won't disappoint him and assureed on behalf of both of them; It didn't make any sense to Violin.

He asked for further clarification. Kartik insisted that Violin could fly back for his work and assured that all was under control and there wasn't anything they were hiding.

Violin didn't know if he should believe him but chose to do so. He booked his flight and told his parents to not talk about it as a gossip mongers or random loose conversation and to let the couple talk.

They didn't like the crude words that Violin used but knew that their old tricks wouldn't work.

Kartik hugged Violin and thanked him for doing what he did.

Violin boarded the taxi and broke down in tears. He bursted crying like he was dying within and didn't know how to manage this and prayed to god to save this family.

Violin couldn't stop tears even after reaching Delhi.

Kartik and Rhea began an honest attempt to learn eachother and open about everything about their lives and how they should be dealing with the situation.

They decided to restart their journey as friends and give their family another chance.

Months passed, Kartik and Rhea had evolved into a more mature relationship and began a true journey to honest and more authentic married life.

Rhea realized that she had come a long way and that she needed to nurture her family and kids even though she continues to hold Vihaan dearly in her life.

Kartik realized that he would have to share the blame along with her parents and he knew that his insecurities won't vanish in a snap but his love for her and kids was stronger. He chose to be her friend in a journey where they both had respect and admired each other.

Rhea realized the magnanimity that Kartik showed along with the fact that nobody could love and do what he did and decided to value this beautiful relationship. Things began turning normal and a happy family got another chance to recontruct.

"WHATEVER HAPPENS ... HAPPENS FOR GOOD"

"LOVE MAY MANIFESTS IN A DIFFERENT FORM .. DON'T DENY YOURSELF TO BE LOVED... ITS ABSENSE HAS TOO MANY YEARNING FOR ONE"

✨✨ Unkahe swaalon Ka jawaab to do..
Unkahi baaton ko awaaz to do... Teri aankhon
mein dekhtey rahe pyaar... Jo hum nahi kar
paaye abhi tak ... Unhe poora karne ka mauka
to do... Iss aag mein jalne se pehle ..Meri
ibaadat ka koi mahr to do... Kehte ho
khush reh... Aur phir khhud ruksat ho jaatey
ho ....humari khushi aap mein hai... Apni dua
ka to ilm karo... Chalo inshallah aapki dua
poori ho...bas allah se guzaarish hai... Mere
janaaze se pehle... Apki dua ki tameel ho...
Allah ki ibaadat ki hai tumhare pyaar mein...
Ussi ibaadat ke naaam par hi... Mujhe apne
pyaar se ameeer to karo... ✨✨✨✨

✨✨✨Inn ankhon ki galti hai... Jo har cheez mein Allah ki Ibaadat aur tere liye Ishq dekhti hai... Ankhein Band ho jayein to darr nahi... Andhere mein bhi tere ishq ki kaynaaat dikhti hai.... Ishq-e-Roohani hai Allah... Mera naaam bhi badnaaami hai.... Mastani mehfil mein... har ghar ka paaani hai... Ali se poooch jisse pata hai har kissson ka... Har kisse mein tera ishq-e-noorani hai. ✨✨✨

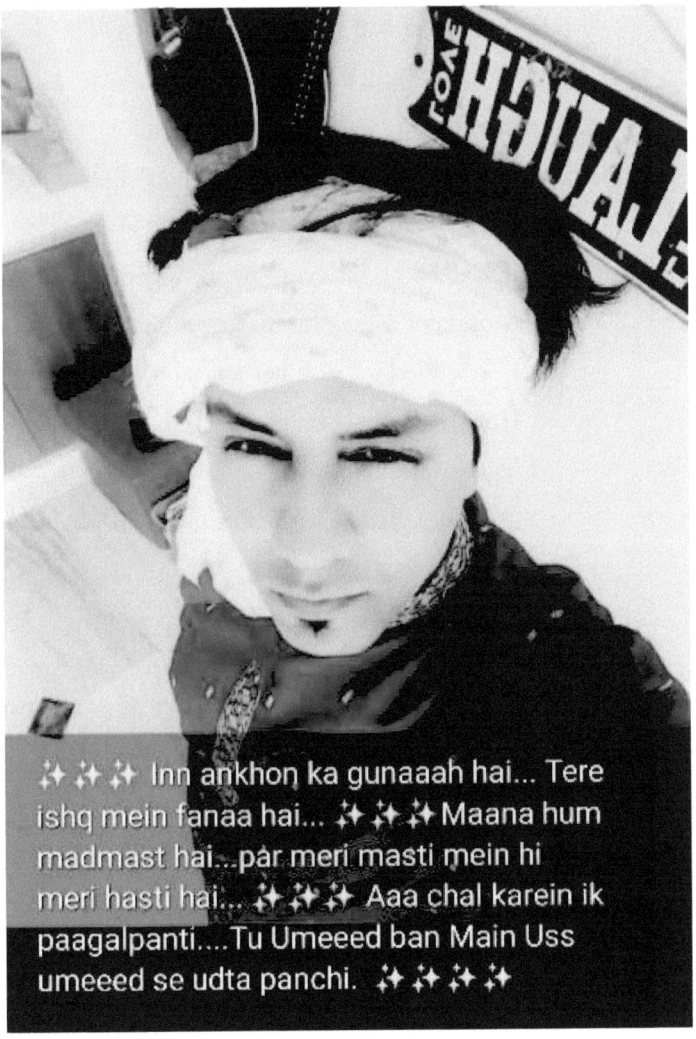

I don't want it anyways

I knew he had his eyes on me
I knew he wanted to hold me tight
He wasn't ready to declare that so soon
He needed to be told that he will be then on top of the moon
He knew he won't be able to hold it tight
But everytime he walked in, his eyes saw the turning on light
The girl kept asking for his attention
He pretended to be in her mansion
But everytime I would walk in
His deep desires will begin talkin
His eyes made every effort to
Contact my eyes
But was careful of what might happen if at all
Really it will meet
The tide of desires will rise and rise
And he would just want to look at me like a child gazing skies
He knew he was falling for me
I smirked and made every effort to raise the bar
The cashier knew what was in making
And he decided to delay my taking
I shook my hair in air dripped in water
And while I tried walking closer to the guy
The drops off my hair blocked his eyes

I moved to hold him and apologise
With the intent to smell his innocent smile
I looked into his eyes and came closer to the lips
He almost froze when I dragged him out and kissed him
Like there was at all nothin
I held his face like a tender kid
And played with his tongue
To never let him forgive
And pushed it in
The heart was beating as fast as sound
And I pulled his hair to let him pound
He moaned so loudly that the cashier came in
And I dropped my hands off him
The guy didn't know if he really wanted to go back
But knew that he wasn't ready to move out of the shack
He walked towards the girl
Living the moment of the possibilities to moan over
I walked out with a smile for I had desired him for long
I knew he can't leave her and ensured now that he won't be able to me either.
I held the coffee in the hands
And the cashier couldn't stop and think
What ought can happen if it happened again!!

Apple of others eyes; kept the doctor away

Ahmir: VID-20170729-WA0016.mp4 (file attached)

Ahmir: Will be going home for dinner.... You come there

Ahmir: Need to meet mum and dad

Ved: VID-20170729-WA0018.mp4 (file attached)

Ahmir: How long will you take

Ved: 10 mins

Ahmir: They are waiting for dinner

Ahmir: Ok

Ved: Taking Taxi

Ved: Pari's husband wants to move out ... can u chk if dere is an opening fr ops mgr

Ved: wherever possible

Ved: Take daaal fr ppl at work

Ved: Atleast they will eat 😛 ☺

Ahmir: Will check with Akshay

Ahmir: Naah

Ahmir: I am not really well so not carrying anything.... Just water and my mug

Ahmir: Not doing so good.... The weather is not good for me

Ahmir: Might get viral fever

Ved: U cld have taken leave

Ved: Why pushing ur self wen u myt get more unwell .... eat as u think ryt ... coffee or tea to remain warm

Ved: Navya was very happy wid how u engaged Avyan

Ved: Avyan kept asking mahesh to give him directions to paint like u were doing here

Ahmir: Ok

Ved: Cold Response

Ahmir: Bad week

Ved: Health or work

Ahmir: Let me concentrate here

Ahmir: Both

Ved: Ok

Ved: I have L&D Conference fr next 3 days early morning so i will leave home by 6am

Ahmir: Ok

Ahmir: So what's the shift timing

Ved: 8am to 5pm bt I will den go to work n b home around 9

Ahmir: Wouldn't that be that a long shift

Ahmir: I might meet Gladys on Saturday

Ahmir: She messaged in the morning and we thought of getting together for a sister date

Ved: Looks like its gonna b way long

Ved: Nt left work

Ved: U enjoy ur sister date

Ahmir: Way long???

Ahmir: Shifts???

Ved: I am just abt to reach home

Ved: Need to wake up

Ved: By 5

Ved: Leave by 6 to reach by 8

Ahmir: Ok

Ahmir: My sister date is canceled

Ved: Y ... we can have a date if u wld like

Ahmir: I am at work again 😌

Ahmir: Batches certification

Ahmir: Monday need to close the batch

Ahmir: Just got a confirmation

Ved: Hmmmm k

Ved: https://youtu.be/PfnwvMbWbX4

Ved: Reached

Ahmir: Good

Ahmir: Enjoy

Ahmir: I am home as well

Ved: IMG-20170801-WA0004.jpg (file attached)

Ahmir: About to sleep

Ahmir: Will make cold coffee

Ahmir: Enjoy your sessions

Ahmir: Where???

Ved: Hahahaha Taj...

Ahmir: Very nice

Ahmir: Have a good buffet

Ved: Hahahaha 😅

Ahmir: Now you have had your breakfast so no more buffets

Ahmir: I sent money to you

Ved: Whatever

Ahmir: Hope you got the message

Ved: Lemmw check....

Ahmir: From now on it will be 8000

Ved: U mad

Ved: Sleep

Ved: it was an insult in the name of breakfast

Ahmir: I just finished the poha and coffee

Ahmir: We waiting if aunty comes

Ahmir: But she is not here

Ahmir: Why what happened

Ved: There was no breakfast

Ahmir: Chai and matthi

Ved: Thy made us run 4 so long here and there

Ved: Now gng to conf

Ved: U sleep

Ahmir: She just left

Ved: Hmmm

Ahmir: Sleeping now

Ved: Ok zzzzz....

Ved: Spoke to Dad

Ved: Leaving from work

Ved: Pari is dropping me in her

Ved: IMG-20170802-WA0011.jpg (file attached)

Ved: IMG-20170802-WA0012.jpg (file attached)

Ved: Sleep

Ved: Gng to work now

Ved: Did u try d shirt

02/08/2017, 5:06 pm - Ahmir: Yeah..... It's big

Ahmir: Also how many sippers did you get

Ved: Way big or fittable

Ved: 2 😭

Ahmir: I saw you left your bag at home there was one in it and they're war one in sink

Ved: Yep i got 2 ....

Ved: U can take d one u want

Ahmir: Ok

Ahmir: Will see

Ahmir: I have my bottle

Ved: 👍

Ved: Manya was here

Ved: N Moti .. the hr guy

Ahmir: Yeah saw the pics

Ahmir: You took the camera

Ved: Yep

Ahmir: I don't know....I thought you mentioned the names of people in your pics

Ahmir: Just read it again.... You mentioned about ANG

Ved: Ohhh ok... naah i was referring to ANG folks

Ved: The pic is diff

Ved: IMG-20170803-WA0000.jpg (file attached)

Ved: IMG-20170803-WA0001.jpg (file attached)

I have transferred 1000 to ur acct. Pls withdraw n give it to house help. She will need it. I have paid rent elec and water as well.

Ahmir: New Doc 2017-08-03.pdf (file attached)

Ved: I have left

Ved: Thank u fr d food and fr dis

Ved: 🙏

Ved: I was talking n u disconnected

Ved: N den not answering

Ved: U said i didnt make smthing or u left hungry ... wen i make smthing wen have u eaten.... i understand ur anger bt u cant generalize and say where is your focus these days and in super anger .... n fr d towel thing I said it coz I was gng to slip n i didnt shout or generalize ... i understand ur anger an am sorry fr doing d lock thing bt i didnt do it deliberately... out of routine I did it and my bad i did it .... nt talking abt is no solution ....

Ved: we shld sten to eachother dan shouting n accusing

Ved: Listen*

Ved: I hear ur situation which is why I didnt say or argue earlier .... atleast give d other person a chance to say

Ahmir: Ved we are again at he said I said

Ahmir: Leave it

Ahmir: Rest

Ahmir: I will see you in the morning at the mosque

Ved: I will bt not talking and keeping within is no solution bt it only piles up ....

Ved: I miss u and i hope u realize it

Ahmir: Ved things are not changing

Ahmir: That is what is happening

Ahmir: This shows that we are both ready with our reasoning

Ahmir: Anyhoo I am not discussing it right now

Ahmir: You go down and eat something

Ved: My back has started aching will sleep rest n eat in d evening

Ved: We need to talk abt it ryt ... widout talking nothing will happen .... nt now will sleep ....

Ved: And dat is ok ... to hear eachother understand and then work to decide wat shld be d case ... we have to maturely discus it.

Ved: U travel safe and eat

Ved: ☹ If wishes were horse, I will ride it and carry you somewhere and take you far away.... i miss alot of things ... bt nt d moment to talk .... u enjoy ur day.

Ved: I found ur ring in clothes ... so its at home ....

Ahmir: Thanks

Ahmir: Did you eat

Ahmir: I am sorry for earlier

Ahmir: I am just not well....mentally I am fucked up

Ved: I did wash sm clothes ....

Ahmir: I need some time for me

Ved: Ok .....

Ahmir: I mean I need to go meditate and just be in a place where I don't know anyone

Ved: U r putting all ur energy at work and work is nt gng to be rewarding

Ahmir: Maybe I need to introspect

Ved: I know and i have been giving u dat

Ahmir: Nooooooo

Ved: U need to unwind n rediscover

Ahmir: No one has been....I need to be alone....I need to be left free for a while

Ved: So how do u wanna do

Ahmir: I don't know

Ahmir: I guess I need to go for a trip

Ahmir: I don't know

Ved: Do u wanna take leaves and be in WeQ ....

Ahmir: Telling you I am fucked up mentally

Ved: U need to talk it out wid somone

Ahmir: No I want to be in a valley where I am the only one

Ved: I did dat ... wid

Ved: Eap ... employee assistance program

Ved: At work

Ahmir: I cant

Ahmir: That's not me

Ved: Then go bt i am nt sure how wld it solve wats within u ... its a break i guess solution

Ved: U need to speak to a neutral person

Ved: Nt talking wont help .... u need to vent ... get sm answrs .... a frsh perspective ....

Ved: N den maybe reenergize

Ahmir: I have been thinking of going out for a week

Ahmir: I guess I need to find myself

Ahmir: I feel lost

Ahmir: And it's me

Ahmir: The ego waala I

Ved: Then u shld go

Ahmir: I feel inferior and I guess I need to re-invent

Ved: Inferior from ppl at work

Ved: ?

Ahmir: Don't know

Ahmir: I feel I am lost

Ved: I will be honest ... n now am nt talking as ur partner bt third party .... u need to speak to smone ... trip n all ... wont fetch u anything until you knw where is d problem... dnt think am giving gyaaan just read like u r hearing for stranger .... u have to have a conversation ... talk ... a new perspective ....

Ahmir: I know but I don't know what I need to talk about

Ahmir: I guess I need a break from life for a while

Ved: U need to be honest to urself.... u knw wat u really want ... or wat is d problem and u knw d solution as well or am sure u can figure it out if u think and evaluate as a third person helping Ahmir.... once u knw wat is it... understand d gravity of d impact and den just do it .... dnt filter d imp ones.... just do it .... like i said if u want a break n travel ... do it.. if u wanna break from me fr smtime and b with mom dad d way u wld want we can explore dat .... i have realized dat i dnt want dat we r resisting eachother bt stil wanting eachother .... we can always talk dis thru ... smtimes such breaks can help u figure out if u want be invested in a relationship or set free ... similar fr anyother relationship with ur friends... we can talk abt us and for any other relationship talk to dat peraon

.... i wld say be true to wat u want and then discuss it wid d person involved wid specific issues n dat is both wanting .... if u were to ask me ... trip is an escape u shld set urself free and seee wat u wld do wen u dnt have to be bound by anyone or anything and do ur normal chores... we can talk later .. u talk to urself n b honest n nail it down to d issue... u knw it more dan .. just talk to urself.

Ahmir: Why you so intelligent...anyways I hope you know I love you and it's a issue that I need to figure out

Ved: Hahaahaha .... yes i knw u love me ..(why i dnt knw 😭) ... n i hope u knw i love u too ... i dnt knw if d intelligent wala was a compliment bt will take it like dat ....

Ved: ☺️ 🙏

Ahmir: Why did we ever grow up

Ahmir: Being kids is fun

Ahmir: That ways it's easy to believe all compliments

Ahmir: No serving thoughts

Ved: Coz dats life baby .... i agree ...

Ved: Its meant to be like dat ...

Ahmir: Love you

Ved: U love krishna ryt ... dis is wat he says

Ahmir: Let me go to class now

Ved: U cant escape life stages

Ved: Love u too

Ved: U have to experience all and enjoy all of dis n suffer to be stronger n wiser .... dats human cycle ... n we r destined .... All planned is gng to happen

Ahmir: Yep.... True that. I guess we are Life

Ved: 👏👏☺️

Ahmir: Anyhoo.... You will be there at mosque

Ved: Yup wat time ...

Ahmir: Will leave by 5:30

Ved: Ok me too

Ved: Mum called

Ved: Gt my cab

Ved: IMG-20170805-WA0026.jpg (file attached)

Ved: Exam gng on

Ved: U take care of urself .... tried waking u to ask if u wanna come bt i gueas u were sleepy.... if possible pls go n visit doc tmrw n nt push urself .... good night love u ...

Ved: I forgot to tell you that it's Ria birthday today

Ved: Do wish her and call her but first take care of yourself and I will see you

Ahmir: I hope your picked up my clothes from the balcony

Ved: Yup i hve

Ahmir: Thanks....I just got up

Ahmir: My stomach was not doing good

Ved: Okies .... u shld eat icecream ... u have been eating kept food n masalas....

Ved: Or just smthing light n see a doc tmrw

Ahmir: I will come early morning

Ahmir: Cause I don't have my keys

Ved: Okies .... no worries... will be leaving ay 12.30 so come as per dat

Ved: Bt do eat now n start to focus on ur health .... hopefully i will get sm kick inspiration from u

Ved: In cab

Ved: Have icecream and not cold coffee ... coffee too much is nt good

Ahmir: Have a good week

Ved: U too

Ahmir: You reached home

Ved: Nope ..... still at work

Ahmir: Why

Ved: Issue with 2 employees ... trying to solve

Ahmir: What are your team members doing..... You doing micro management

Ahmir: Anyhoo

Ahmir: Did you eat

Ved: This is my class .... me trg ... all trainers booked 😖

Ved: I did

Ahmir: Ok

Ved: U

Ahmir: I had

Ved: Okies good .... wat hw is ur tummy

Ved: Leavin noq

Ved: Now

Ahmir: Good

Ved: Hm

Ahmir: Getting breakfast and leaving in sometime

Ahmir: Just left

Ved: In cab

Ved: Work time

Ahmir: In cab... Overslept

Ved: Wow .... bt u wld b fresh now

Ved: Hope u reached

Ved: Have back to back sessions will b late tdy as well

Ahmir: Just reached

Ahmir: Have you left

Ved: Nope

Ved: will leqve by 1.15

Ahmir: Ok

Ahmir: Did you eat

Ved: I did like sooo fast bt dats ok....

Ahmir: Listen you want to go out over the weekend..... Saturday, Sunday, Monday

Ahmir: I can stay back for a day or two and you come back

Ahmir: Though I don't have the money

Ahmir: So it's wishful thinking

Ved: We can plan smthing ... lemme check mndy n all plan

Ahmir: Ok

Ved: Left

Ved: Gt my cab

Ahmir: Travel safely

Ved: Yup .... u eat n rest well

Ved: Bt get up on time

Ved: 🙂 😬

Ahmir: The flush was pressed I guess it never came up after you last used

Ahmir: There is no water in the tank now

Ahmir: Nothing for me to even wash my bum

Ved: Huh

Ved: I actually had full motor and tank gt full n den i went to washroom

Ved: Am at work

Ved: My bad sorry

Ahmir: No worries

Ahmir: It's full again

Ved: Ok grt

Ahmir: Going for a shower now

Ved: Ok ....

Ved: Om my way home

Ahmir: Good

Ahmir: Rest well

Ved: Home

Ved: Boarded

Ved: Work time

Ved: Where r u

Ved: Pari is blessed with baby boi

Ahmir: I am at home

Ahmir: Had a little fever

Ved: Ohhhh ok

Ved: Left

Ved: Did u take medZ

Ahmir: Yeah

Ved: Gng to meet Pari on my way

Ahmir: Ok

Ahmir: Give my blessings

Ved: Will do

Ved: At work

Ahmir: Now??

Ved: At 5

Ahmir: Ok

Ahmir: I have reached as well

Ved: Am home

Ved: Gt my cab

Ved: I saw 3 missed calls from u

Ved: Hello???????

Ahmir: That ws in the morning

Ved: Ok.

.. hve u lft

Ahmir: I am home

Ved: Me on d way

Ved: I left my earfones... will take it tmrw

Ahmir: Ok

Ahmir: Sleep well

Ved: U too

Ahmir: Get up

Ved: I am up

Ahmir: Ok

Ahmir: What time are you coming home

Ved: 11.30

Ahmir: Ok

Ved: Am at class

Ahmir: Ok

Ahmir: I am at shopping center buying some groceries

Ved: Ohhh ok

Ahmir: Had to go to Subhash Nagar......DC was very crowded

Ved: Ok

Ahmir: How long will you take

Ved: Will be dere in 10 mins

Ahmir: Ok

Ahmir: I am home

Ved: Ok me waiting

Ved: Left

Ahmir: Good.... Enjoy

Ahmir: https://youtu.be/Ee_I_SGu1Gc

Ahmir: Practice your Spanish

Ved: Yea ryt

Ved: Am at work

Ahmir: Good

Ahmir: Have a good week

Ahmir: She why not

Ahmir: It's in Spanish

Ahmir: I went out to sardar uncle age hit stuff to eat

Ahmir: IMG-20170813-WA0003.jpg (file attached)

Ved: U too

Ved: Yep bt need better way

Ved: I may get shortlisted fr a play at institiute

Ved: Nt sure

Ved: Nice

Ved: I knw u asked to go fr a trip

Ved: If u wanna go alone go ahead .. coz wid Pari nt here ... i will have to watch my leaves

Ved: N cant take leaves frm classes

Ved: Or we plan later in sept or oct..

Ahmir: I can't take leaves as well

Ahmir: Not at least this week

Ahmir: Very good and I hope it hapoens

Ahmir: You will become a celeb then

Ved: Its a play for practise... wat celen

Ved: Celeb*

Ved: If u get leaves ... u shld go... maybe a solo trip will help to build perspective.... i still feel u want to spend time wid urself n dat gives u peace

Ahmir: I dunno.....I think of I go alone....I will loose you

Ahmir: There is a fear

Ahmir: Also I have forgotten how to spend on me.... You have been doing that for so long

Ahmir: I guess I am only used of molesting you

Ved: See here is wat i think ... d fear of loosing me is making u loose urself n it is impacting 'us'.... besides am nt gng anywhere ... it makes u value d other person... maybe we need to have open relationship .... may be we need to rejuvenate ourselves and rediscover wat we want ... am nt gng anywhere n neither r u ... bt letting eachone open.. it wld hell us value ourselves ...

Ved: And besides baby ... wld u want to be wid me n remain unhappy or be wid me n still keep urself happy or nt be wid me and b happy... d intent shld be we r happy n spread happiness. .... maybe we need to know ourselves more ....

Ahmir: I think we need to talk.... Because of lately it seems we both are scared somewhat but at the same we are aware of letting each other go???

Ahmir: I don't know

Ahmir: I am so confused...I am not saying things don't irritate me.... You know they do and I know I almost kill you everyday

Ved: Yup we shld talk wid an open mind and everything

Ved: I feel I holding u .... i love u bt am controlling ur actions....

Ved: Agree there r things dat r irritating and we r holding dem inside only to know dat it erupts one day ....

Ahmir: But what's happening to us is something that's rather strange

Ahmir: Do you want me to move in to the next room

Ved: See we r evolving as adults and we r more aware of wat we want to do .... i think u have been restricted by me and by urself fr ur love fr me ... bt dat is pushing u away more dan getting closer .... and same goes wid me .... we r making peace wid our presence bt no convo ....

Ved: Naaaaah ....

Ved: I think u need ur freedom uncontrolled and i need mine while we dnt want to let go or leave us

Ved: And dat needs an open discussion ....

Ved: D ques is ... do u want to let go off me
.... do u feel u wld be better off me... or do u think we shld b be wid eachother as a commitment bt let eachother free ....

Ved: Loving eachother shld mean we wanna b and are happy around eachother ... we love eachother bt we r making peace wid not having eachother around

Ved: Lets talk ... 🙂

Ved: Am in cab n its drizzling crazy

Ahmir: Reading all of it it seems I am the only one with issues

Ahmir: I don't know what's in your mind

Ved: I was just gng to call u n talk

Ved: See i have my own concerns ....

Ved: Bt if i share mine too

Ved: Then who will listen

Ved: To whom

Ved: N we both knw our issues

Ahmir: But I don't know yours

Ved: Wat do u think

Ahmir: Ved you know I don't like these games

Ahmir: If only I knew why would I ask

Ved: Ok

Ved: Lemme tell u

Ahmir: Be honest and don't try and sugar coat anything

Ved: I will be honest

Ved: First u dnt have time for me ... u r way too invested in fone work sleep dat dere is no us ... now ur definition of us time spending is diff n mine is diff

Ved: Second our intimacy is almost zero .... fr me its very imp... i cant even flirt wid u .. fr i dnt see u reciprocate

Ved: Third u have yearn fr cleanliness i try wat i can do ... bt u dnt appreciate wat i do bt only wat i miss

Ved: Fourth ... u question urself alot and u compare n den bother urself ... so smtimes i feel if i share smthing good u wld nt like it ....

Ved: Fifth .... i have this feeling u dnt need me except the fact that u have me .... ur sense of care is very silent effort bt nothing beyond dat ...

Ved: Its funny

Ved: Fr u may laugh

Ved: I even thought u changed ur orientation

Ahmir: Yes I am laughing here.... But rest I understand.

Ahmir: I can do everything but change my orientation

Ved: I know bt u knw smtimes wen smone wants mental stimulus only

Ved: It doesnt matter

Ved: Fr me i think we have made peace wid our problems bt we havent internally and r struggling

Ved: N i can only think of things dat i shared as solutions

Ved: I even kept my own personal fears aside ... coz honestly i dnt want that we live wid d fear bt not be happy and bring d best

Ved: So here is me

Ahmir: Hmmmmmm

Ahmir: You know I love you..... But you also know that I love myself even more. I am a stubborn ass man. I guess I am struggling with this

Ved: I know u love me

Ved: I love u too ...

Ahmir: Do I do what I want to or what I am being wanted to.....

Ahmir: As I said....I feel I have lost myself

Ved: I know u r stubborn as well

Ved: N i have made peace wid it bt am nt ok with us suppressing eachother

Ved: N i dnt want us to reach a situation where we push eachother to reach d extreme stage

Ved: I am becoming carefree n i have realized i cant change u fr u r a man of ur own principles

Ved: U shld do wat gives u happiness

Ved: See of all i knw u

Ved: U live on relationships and care fr dem

Ved: N u want to take care of alot of them and do ur best

Ved: Sm maynt anymore coz of me

Ved: And sm coz they r married etc 3tc

Ved: U miss d free bird u were bt den i think if i wasnt there u wld be sleeping fr u love sleeping since we met

Ved: U have given all ur effort to work fr ryt reasons bt dat also u r nt ok wid me and den its me who doesnt live upto ur expectations

Ved: So maybe d love is fr ur own love fr me

Ved: Or u love ur zeal to love smome

Ahmir: Are you saying I don't love YOU

Ahmir: It reads that ways

Ved: I am saying i dnt knw why u love me ...

Ved: Naaah its like wid all d misery i have led fr u ... y wld anyone love

Ved: I kmw d reasons why i love u ...

Ved: Am home n pooping ...

Ahmir: You think you are the only one with driving miseries

Ahmir: I have given you enough trouble

Ahmir: The more I talk the more I feel that we both have become different people in last four years.... And I guess the fight has raised that self learn if not anything

Ahmir: I know I have changed some and more or less I am the same man

Ahmir: But it's either too much life and little too much expectation.... From each other or from life that I am questioning.... Am I doing right by you

Ahmir: I see that I have done nothing but taken advantage of you

Ved: See my reasons to love u and be mad abt r clear ... they r nt overlapping ...

Ved: I dnt think n i genuinely feel ....

Ahmir: Same here

Ved: Yes and i am to be blamrd fr d change

Ved: A lot more

Ved: There r other reasons as well

Ved: We have become more clearer fr wat we want

Ahmir: I don't know what you want..... And that kills me

Ahmir: Cause I don't know

Ved: And more aware wid wat kinda person we wanna be... d challenge is d other person. Is nt ok wid wat

Ved: Wat do u want ...

Ahmir: See we keep asking each other

Ahmir: We are scared

Ved: Wat r u scared abt

Ahmir: But we both want the same thing

Ahmir: We want to be with ourselves for a while

Ahmir: But we want to be in each others lives as well

Ahmir: I know I do

Ved: Hahahahah

Ahmir: For you are inseparable part of me

Ved: Honestly this is wat i think

Ved: I cant let go off u

Ahmir: Matlab

Ved: Simple

Ved: Dat was a dialogue .. funsake

Ahmir: See there is never funsake with you

Ahmir: I know you well enough

Ved: Dnt read too much

Ved: If i have been honest untill now

Ved: I wont spoil it wid sm starters

Ahmir: Author saheb you are not the one to waste words

Ved: I think we need time from eachpther....

Ved: N rediscover d love

Ahmir: But what will I do

Ahmir: I have forgotten how to spend on me

Ved: So all d more

Ved: Go spend on u

Ahmir: You have always....

Ved: Naah u spend on ur hair cut

Ved: Leh trips were

Ved: Bothways

Ahmir: I am in my sleep too dependent on you

Ahmir: Not the way you want me to..... Bit in my own way

Ved: See all of dat shld remain dere to make a relationship exist n remain strong

Ved: U r bigger author dan me ...

Ahmir: Yeah right

Ved: Wid ur abstract thoughts

Ahmir: What

Ved: Wat do u think is d way out ...

Ahmir: Don't know if it was compliment or you being sarcastic

Ved: It was a compliment

Ahmir: I guess we need to have a common goal

Ahmir: Take up something together

Ved: We tried ...spanish

Ved: I even thought marriage counselling

Ved: Bt i guess at dis moment

Ahmir: That moves us both and makes us better.... mentally, physically, socially

Ved: Anything to put us together will push us away

Ahmir: And then we need to have our own goals too

Ved: See fr all of dat we need to knw ourselves ..n wat we want

Ahmir: You need to have your support center and I need to have mine

Ved: We r nt even sure wat do we really want

Ahmir: How about we both take one trip each

Ahmir: Alone

Ved: See here also its like i dnt want to feel bad so u also take

Ved: Dis is my recommendation

Ahmir: Wherever..... No one asking our wanting the other to follow

Ved: Fr d trip ... u go alone

Ahmir: Noooooo it's not that I will feel bad

Ahmir: See I am scared because I know me

Ved: Scared of wat

Ahmir: I can very easily get used to running alone

Ved: Boi den dat means u r nt being true to urself

Ved: D problem wont change

Ahmir: If I get one ......I might start taking trips all by myself

Ahmir: You not understanding

Ahmir: I am not saying if I take a trip alone you have to take one too

Ved: Maybe we gove eachother 1 month 2 months like a break from eachother ... and am seriously putting this n den maybe evaluate wat works fr us and how

Ahmir: No

Ved: Arey i knw wat is ur fear

Ved: Dat u wld be used to

Ved: Trips alone

Ahmir: Break how

Ved: Now dat needs discussion

Ved: Maybe u do want u want ... i do wat i want ...

Ahmir: What do you mean by break.....I asked.... Do you want me to move out....I will in the next room

Ved: Arey baba its nt moving out or in

Ved: Do as u wish ... n no need to tell or talk to each other except wen home ... try n spend time away

Ahmir: Ok I gotta run right now..... Anit is calling

Ved: Keep sm basics cleanliness

Ved: Ok

Ahmir: Hahahahaha.....I should start working with MCD

Ved: Lol

Ved: Tell him u r busy n talking

Ahmir: I am a freak....I fight with mum, bhaabhi everyone

Ved: Or else full circle

Ved: Convo again

Ahmir: It's not that I pick on you

Ahmir: Separate

Ved: U fyt wid urself also

Ved: I knw bt i need

Ahmir: For cleaning....naah. I sometimes let go

Ved: Sm appreciation

Ved: Hahah

Ved: Maybe wen we redicsocver ourselves we will knw wat we want ....

Ved: We shld be happy together bt if we r happier wid ourselves den we r like those couples who r stuck coz of traditions ...

Ahmir: Chal you eat abhi

Ved: Hahaha I am

Ved: Chutni

Ahmir: Kadhi and sabzi are there in the fridge

Ved: N sticks

Ahmir: And rice to

Ved: Oh ok

Ved: I didnt see will check fridge

Ved: Will talk later wen u come

Ahmir: Don't eat this....Usually you have issues with eating parantha and now eating butter bread

Ved: Bt we had a mature discussion m we shld just keep doing dat

Ved: Buter

Ved: ??

They r sticks

Ahmir: Yeah the next thing I tell you is I have to come to work early

Ahmir: Lo

Ved: U shld marry smome at work ....

Ved: Find a girl

Ved: I can be ur misstress

Ahmir: Hahhahhahaha

Ved: Am telling u all problems solved

.. ...

Ahmir: Why don't you do it

Ahmir: You anyways my sugar boy candy

Ved: Naaah ....

Ahmir: I can't be your sugar daddy

Ved: Am nt ... u r spending more coz pf me ... debt has increased ....

Ved: U dnt be my sugar daddy

Ahmir: I wish

Ahmir: That's all on me

Ahmir: You had nothing to do with it

Ved: I led u too... u r paying rent u dnt hve too..u hv apts

Ved: Den leave early

Ahmir: No one did anything to anyone.... We both live our lives and we have our own debts

Ahmir: Let's not blame ourselves

Ved: Yup alot of it ... 😊 ....

Ved: I ate and nw scratching myseld fr its hot ...

Ahmir: No electricity?

Ved: Its there .. bt i think d flies or i need to take shower

Ahmir: I guess you need a hot water bath

Ahmir: You might be missing it

Ahmir: Go for a spa

Ved: Lol...

Ved: I took desi shower fr nw

Ahmir: No I know how you love a hot water shower

Ahmir: And since you have moved..... You have been deprived of it

Ahmir: Sleep now

Ahmir: I might leave in sometime

Ved: Naaah am good .... just watching videos

Ved: Will sleep while watching

Ved: Songs

Ahmir: Now practice that spanish

Ved: Need attentiom ... 15th is leave so will b closing alot of such things ... have home work as well

Ahmir: https://youtu.be/37jSVy-9FOs

Ahmir: Watch this

Ahmir: Says your katha

Ved: Well put together ....

Ved: Gt my cab ....

Ved: Cldnt talk wen u came ... lets talk tonyt

Ahmir: Don't sweat.... Enjoy your day

Ahmir: You left early

Ved: Yep a trainer is nt in... class needs to b handled

Ved: Its imp dat we talk or all of this will keep cropping up

Ved: Am at work

Ahmir: At work

Ved: Enjoy ur day

Ahmir: IMG-20170814-WA0003.jpg (file attached)

Sharin and I went next door...a new cafe has opened

Ved: Nice

Ahmir: I will go home in the morning.... Asked mum to buy me a kurta for tomorrow so will go and pick it up

Ahmir: You had your dinner

Ved: U r working tmrw??

Ahmir: Yep

Ahmir: No leave....else would have made some plans

Ahmir: IMG-20170814-WA0004.jpg (file attached)

Ved: Nice

Ved: Jst left

Ahmir: Very long shift

Ved: Yup ... interviews

Ahmir: Hope you ate and now sleep

Ved: Still on way ... ate samosa

Ahmir: Just left with office cab

Ahmir: Will go to c4

Ahmir: You get something to eat when you come home and get my kurta

Ahmir: And sleep

Ahmir: Aunty will come and I will ask her to wash clothes

Ved: How come ur plan changed 360 degree

Ahmir: Nothing changed

Ahmir: I can still come

Ahmir: Infact I am coming home

Ahmir: I just thought you will do hurry to go back in the morning

Ahmir: And since you are there I thought you can pick up the kurta

Ahmir: I was only going to pick that up

Ved: ☺

Ahmir: What emoji

Ved: Dunno wat to say or even think

Ahmir: Why

Ved: Coz its weird ... u say r gng to c4 den saying u r cmmg here .... u only cmng to pick ur stuff den u want me to get it n now u r coming ... why d confusion... besides if u were leaving dat early i cld have waited fr dats wat i asked u .. u said u wld come in morning

Ved: So dunno wat to aay

Ved: Say

Ahmir: Ved I guess you read too much into it....m did not want you to wait for this long so asked you to go home...... It's been a very long day she I left early cause again have to be there early tomorrow.....

Ahmir: Anit told me to go home cause none of us could find the data and need to connect with the mis team

Ahmir: Cause very sleepy and have to go early I thought I will get drop at c4

Ahmir: I had to go to Mum only to pick up my kurta which I realized that you can bring too

Ahmir: Now this is the whole thing... Dunno what you thinking

Ahmir: Anyways I am about to reach

Ved: I said d same thing i dunno wat to say or wat to think

Ahmir: See you in five

Ahmir: You go to sleep

Ved: I want to watch d speech so not gng to sleep

Ahmir: That's in two or so hours

Ved: Yep

Ahmir: Dad will wake you up

Ved: Naah i will be restless wid such sleep

ed: Will b fine

Ved: Am at c4

Ved: <Some Promo code text>

Ahmir: You could have come home to eat

Ahmir: I just got ready... Going in a bit

Ahmir: Coming home in a bit

Ahmir: Eating something

Ved: Okies .... i dont feel like eating feeling gaseous ...

Ved: Will have milk later

Ahmir: Mum has packed for you

Ved: I was thinking of jst milk

Ahmir: Will add to the acidity

Ahmir: In cab

Ved: Trvl safe

Ahmir: You rest and if you can get some small potatoes and tomatoes.... Also order water

Ved: Ok

Ved: Gng out to eat ... lets see

Ahmir: Eat well

Ved: You deleted this message

Ved: You deleted this message

Ahmir: Deleted messages??

Ahmir: You wanna say something

Ved: Generally alot abt our convo... bt this was incorrect msg... i was sending to ria ...

Ahmir: Ok

Ahmir: Did you eat

Ved: Yep now making tea

Ved: I have lost my debit card... have blocked it ... so cldnt buy anything... i will transfer money to ur acct so if u cld widraw n gimme

Ahmir: Where did you loose it any idea

Ahmir: When did you see that last

Ahmir: You should have called mum to get money

Ahmir: So you didn't eat anything???

Ved: No idea ... wen i went down i saw my wallet n it wasnt dere searchd bt no hlp

Ved: I used my cc ...

Ahmir: Good at least you ate

Ahmir: Baby you ok

Ved: I ate bt lost ...no trnx dn so allok

Ved: M ok

Ahmir: What

Ved: Card lost ... cld custmr servc ... chckd to see any debit no debit unknown done

Ved: IMG-20170816-WA0000.jpg (file attached)

Ahmir: You don't need to transfer

Ahmir: I can still get the money

Ahmir: I just left.... Couldn't find the lock to the balcony so just bolted the door.

Ved: Ohhh it was at d bed

Ved: Travel safe

Ahmir: At work now

Ved: Njoy

Ved: Left

Ahmir: Travel safely

Ahmir: Do you have money or should I get more

Ved: I do .... didnt use mch

Ahmir: Let me know and I will get those

Ved: Ok thanks

Ved: Gt my cab

Ved: I hve asked d water guy to cm

Ved: Kept mney near speakers

Ahmir: I had the money

Ahmir: You should have taken the money with you

Ahmir: Anyhoo...... Have a good day

Ahmir: You left really early today

Ved: Workshop

Ved: Reached

Ved: U sounded diff on d fone

Ahmir: Different..... How

Ahmir: I was walking in to a meet

Ved: Tone .... i may have misread it.... np

Ved: R ur ppl cmng tmrw

Ahmir: Nope

Ved: Ok

Ved: Left

Ahmir: Travel safely

Ved: Yup

Ved: Had a very insightful convo wid d head ....

Ahmir: Ok

Ahmir: About

Ved: His relationship wid his wife 🙂

Ahmir: Hmmmmm

Ahmir: Going to mum..... Else i will sleep the whole day

Ahmir: I have reached home.... See you here.... Dont keep sleeping till late.... Come and eat on time and rest here

Ved: Ok

Ved: Rechd

Ahmir: Sleep well and take proper rest

Ved: Yp ... u too

Ahmir: How are you feeling now

Ahmir: Did not come for breakfast

Ved: Better ... i am having soup ... will need to become very careful of myself . Health

Ahmir: Go get a checkup done first

Ahmir: Its not what you thinking

Ved: I anyways need to feel fitter ... i dnt ...

Ahmir: Its bad sitting posture and muscle pull

Ahmir: Soup from??

Ved: Cld b bt i am nt gng to eat anything fried ... i need to move to a heslthy diet and my body needs a big change ...

Ved: Made wid tomatos n brocli

Ahmir: Consult a dietician or a doctor and devise a diet

Ahmir: Doing on your own you will miss the nourish

Ahmir: I am not saying don't do it.... But have a plan and from an approved authority

Ved: Lemme me madly into it ....

Ahmir: ?????

Ved: I mean .. i need to push myself .. d dietacian who i consulted

Ved: Will pick dat diet

Ved: Btw ... d cooler is gone

Ved: Also i will transfer mny to ur acct

Ved: Pls if u cld withdraw

Ahmir: What do you mean its gone

Ahmir: Has it stopped working totally or is not pulling water

Ved: I was sleeping ... I smelled smthing was burning and saw d cooler stopped ...

Ved: Both

Ahmir: Ok

Ahmir: Dont transfer any money

Ved: Why

Ahmir: I will withdraw anyways.... How much do you need

Ahmir: I will take it from you later when I need it

Ved: No pls ....

Ved: I need to give 500 to aunty tmrw ... n 500 so i will ransfer 1000

Ved: I have reached

Ahmir: Have a good class

Ved: Thank u

Ved: Hw r things

Ved: How did it happen...

Ved: My condolences

Ahmir: Just finished the cremation

Ahmir: Was very old and sick... 81

Ved: Aaaaah k ....

Ved: So d family was prepaared....

Ahmir: Not really.... We thought he would stay for couple of months

Ahmir: ... But yes in a way

Ahmir: I am home

Ahmir: I have two questions

Ahmir: You got time??

Ahmir: Won't take long

Ved: Sure ....

Ahmir: Did mum and dad talk to you about the cooler?

Ved: Wen can we talk

Ahmir: Give me half hour.... Will call you

Ved: K

Ahmir: Tried calling the number was switched off

Ahmir: Missed voice call

Ved: Was charging n just rechead

Ved: Trying to call u nw bt ur fone is nt reachable

Ved: Can u come home early

Ahmir: IMG-20170822-WA0008.jpg (file attached)

Ved: Thank u

Ahmir: Its this the one

Ved: Yes

Ahmir: I need some time to pack and go.... Can i take two days?

Ved: Yes .... this is ur house as much as its mine....

Ahmir: Thank you

Ved: 🙏

Ahmir: I love you

Ved: Den dnt leave

Ahmir: Always

Ved: Hmmmm

Ahmir: You know it.....

Ved: We r just being mad ... i knw dat too

Ahmir: Have a good day at work.... And promise you will eat as well

Ved: I have to stop promising

Ved: Promises r meant to be broken

Ahmir: Then take it as one of the last requests of mine

Ahmir: Eat on time and take care of yourself

Ved: Cant give u dat ....

Ahmir: For mum and dad if not for me

Ved: God will take care of me

Ved: He has and he will

Ved: I love dem

Ved: Pls tell dem i always dere fr dem

Ved: N dis promise i am giving u

Ahmir: Dont give me anything baby..... We have given each other everything..... Its for mum and dad in Punjab as well

Ved: Its ok

Ved: 🙂

Ahmir: Be good

Ved: 🙂

Ahmir: 😊

Ved: 🙂

Ahmir: I don't wanna go home

Ved: Dnt den

Ahmir: Dont stress yourself

Ahmir: I think i have gone mad

Ved: Where r u

Ved: Take a leave and rest

Ahmir: I have to go to my uncle really in the morning and seek back home late.... You make sure you eat and leave on time

Ahmir: I am good.....

Ved: Bt u wld hamper ur own health Ahmir

Ved: I will do eat

Ahmir: Let it be Ved

Ahmir: Its anyways not a time of merriment

Ved: Merriment??

Ahmir: Joy

Ved: Taking care of ur heslth isnt joy ...

Ved: And nobody is having joy

Ved: Bt u need rest

Ved: Or go late

Ahmir: True..... But our lives need to move forward. I don't have leaves to take. I am on leave tomorrow

Ahmir: And need to do a training

Ved: U wanted me to take leaves next week

Ahmir: Yeah

Ved: U take rest ... i will stress u

Ved: N den u r saying u dnt hsve leaves

Ved: Its ok... u rest

Ved: I love u watever happens

Ahmir: The more I think on it.... The more I feel we will hurt

Ahmir: I will pack

Ahmir: We both have to live the pain

Ved: Talk to mum

Ved: She will guide u n eventually us

Ved: Hero i love u .... and maybe we need to rediscover love fr eachother ....

Ved: 🤝

Ahmir: And that's why I have packed my stuff..... Unless we loose we won't find. I will just have run away from a lot of stuff to rediscover it all.

Ved: U r nt smone I want to loose .... so maybe if i let u go now bt i win u after dat ..... i think dat will be us winning

Ved: Love u .... and now i dnt want us to cry bt love d moment

Ahmir: I am sorry Ved i could not be what you hoped for.... Infact I drove you crazy hell

Ahmir: Yet i dont regret that

Ahmir: I made you my kinda crazy

Ved: Boi i dnt regret .... i am crazy already and i love d crazy us ....

Ved: Lets nt be sad

Ahmir: Love you too..... Forever and a day

Ved: Dnt b sorry

Ved: And i doo too

Ved: We r gonna hurt ourselves bt we need to redicosver

Ved: I love u fr u fulfil my soul

Ved: And u always will .... nobody can make dat soul connection wid me

Ved: So i fyt n watever bt i find peace in u

Ved: We need to find peace

Ved: Rediscover and love ourselves and den we may get

Ved: N redisc9ver us

Ved: 😍 and maybe i can flirt wid u more

Ahmir: Lets live and keep us healthy... Even if it is to meet again and kill each other. Don't know about flirting

Ved: Hahahahah we will

Ved: Maybe we will be mistresses of eachother

Ved: Or platonic connection

Ved: Untill we learn fire in belly and btw us

Ved: N our individual lives

Ahmir: I will make a time table for you and leave .

Ved: Whatever... atleast give me a reason to disturb

Ahmir: Don't follow it

Ved: Lol

Ahmir: And eat beyond stuff

Ved: I need to get d sexier me out ....

Ahmir: Indulge in arts and plays

Ahmir: Hahahhahajajhaja

Ved: U too .... indulge in fotography painting dancing and travel ... read 😬

Ahmir: If only you could see your soul.... Its sexy enough

Ved: Hahahahha soul is the only sexy.... body sexy makes me more sexier

Ahmir: As for your books.... I have read the life of it.... You anyways gave my copy away 😊

Ved: My next book*

Ved: Ur copy is dere

Ved: Besides u dnt read it

Ahmir: Lets not fight on that now

Ved: Lol

Ved: 😁 😁 🤩

Ahmir: Maybe we take time and start going out in dates again with each other

Ved: Yep.... and many more ...

Ahmir: Ohhhh no

Ved: Wat

Ahmir: Many more....

Ahmir: One is good

Ahmir: Rest thank god for friends and family

Ved: Lol.. i meant more ways to meet

Ved: Yup

Ahmir: Yeah thats good

Ved: Perfecto

Ved: U come n see my play

Ved: If i clear

Ahmir: I will

Ahmir: And you will

Ved: Hahahahah lets see ....

Ahmir: Just keep me informed

Ved: I cant even remember my dialogues

Ved: Ofcorse

Ahmir: What's the play about

Ved: Am playing Damian .... its a thriller ....

Ved: Murder myserty

Ahmir: Hahahhahaha

Ahmir: Kill me

Ahmir: Find out who did it

Ahmir: You will remember everything

Ved: God protects us

Ahmir: Read the whole message

Ved: Lol paaagal

Ved: U don't know i have killer instincts

Ahmir: Well i guess we all do

Ahmir: That's why i stopped cooking 😂

Ahmir: Btw there is one milk packet in fridge .... Finish it or it will go bad

Ahmir: Lets give time to work right now....i will have to go early morning tomorrow

Ahmir: So need to finish work on time

Ahmir: I have reached work

Ved: Okies ....

Ved: Yea ryt

Ved: Yep

Ved: Enjoy n eat

Ahmir: Well.... A lot of fresh mind to eat here today

Ved: Hahahahah ... enjoy munching

Ved: Seeing ur bag here made me realize I cant imagine my life widout u .... we have our differences bt how can i let my soul leave me .... u wanna move fr sm days to b3a ... move bt come back .... Ahmir our love needs strength at dis time.... i dnt think we were meant to part ways .... plssssssssssss i am beging

Ved: U knnw me more den my parents

Ved: PTT-20170822-WA0015.opus (file attached)

Ved: I cant Ahmir .... i will die ....

Ved: Plssss

Ahmir: You wont

Ved: Plssss i beg .... dnt

Ahmir: Remember our promise to each other

Ved: I dnt care abt promise Ahmir

Ved: U r more dan any of my differences

Ved: I cant imagine life widout

Ved: U

Ved: Plssss

Ved: Am trembling here

Ved: I whole soul is shaken

Ved: I cant let u go

Ved: We will do everything together; dying fighting eating

Ved: Bt i cant

Ved: Let u go

Ved: Even fr a another thought

Ved: I feel like slapping myself right now

Ahmir: Don't Ved

Ahmir: Dont

Ahmir: I did this in the morning and you are doing it now

Ahmir: We are facing the heart ache

Ved: Ahmir plssssss.... We have gone mad

Ahmir: We have to see that..... If we are making a mistake then we will be guided back to each other

Ved: Ahmir isnt just a bf bt my soul

Ved: U r nt getting d magnitude

Ahmir: We will have to do this madness or else we will loose ourselves and turn the other person into mad

Ahmir: Lets get some distance

Ahmir: I am

Ved: U want to stay away from me

Ved: Do dat

Ved: Bt i want u back

Ahmir: Thats why i called you in the morning and did this

Ved: Ahmir u r my

Ved: Soul

Ved: Nt even better half

Ved: I had gone mad advising you all that shit

Ved: I should be hit with shoes

Ahmir: Both of us should be hit

Ved: No Ahmir.. No

Ved: We are doing madness.. sheer madness lets not do this

Ved: I wont let it happen

Ved: To you and myself

Ved: Boii... You are my husband ... hit me with anything

Ved: Bt dnt drop me.....

Ved: I will take everyone's life for you... just don't take away my life.... I need my Ahmir

Ved: U want us to move back

Ved: To b3a

Ved: I will do it i dnt care

Ved: U want me to take leaves lets run away ....

Ved: I want u to cm n hit me hard fr even thinking of letting u go

Ved: I want to hit u fr even letting me go ....

Ahmir: Ved stop it

Ved: Yes Ahmir... lets stop d madness

Ahmir: We are hurting each other

Ahmir: And as we said in the afternoon.... We need to have this space

Ved: Yaaar if we love eachpther we will also hurt ....

Ahmir: Its our lives and it will hurt

Ved: Ahmir we have gone mad... we want to live this ulta metro life .... we r nt these ppl.....

Ved: We need space?? How much space? Humein space chahiye ... Instead we need to kill the space

Ved: Ahmir dnt think am just getting emotional .....

Ved: I dnt knw if u get me

Ved: Bt Ahmir is a bf of Ved

Ved: Isnt just a bf*

Ved: Ahmir is Veds soul n conscious...

Ved: This isn't just a roadside affair boi..

Ved: It happened… And left

Ved: We need to work towards killing the space within… so much so that nobody dares to create space again

Ved: IMG-20170823-WA0000.jpg (file attached)

Wat is dis ??? This is divine Ahmir .... a husband and a husband .... doing things like a normal married couple... who does dis

Ved: Dis is a family ... a fsmily of 2 ... a family of 2 and 4 parents

Ved: ??

Ahmir: Dont make it difficult Ved

Ahmir: This wasn't roadside and can never be

Ved: So den lets nt treat it like dat

Ahmir: But its hurting us right now

Ved: U have differences i have

Ahmir: I am not

Ved: This is some madness in the head

Ved: There is nothing which we cant fix ... nothing like that has happened.

Ved: Why should we think negative

Ahmir: Nothing negative

Ved: To den why cant we work .... We have given eachother enough space

Ved: Now we need to reduce it

Ved: Such soul connection doesn't happens in married couples

Ved: Wen i entered home ... My soul was ripped apart... i didnt hsve d courage to open ... i opened

Ved: N saw

Ved: N den i was like wat the hell am doing

Ved: Everything looked so petty to me in front of my love my soul

Ahmir: Ved.... You facing the same shock that I felt in the. Morning

Ved: And am talking abt my own

Ved: Ahmir pls dnt think

Ahmir: We have to face these fears....

Ved: I was in shock

Ved: I am in shock

Ahmir: The core issues the things we have said to each other...... Words i have said to you

Ved: Shocked dat we have let such issues take over

Ahmir: They can't be taken back

Ved: They cant be taken back bt who can say it

Ahmir: You may forget them i can't

Ved: Only to one i love d most

Ved: Who is telling to forget

Ahmir: And i guess thats why i humbly request...... Lets be open to this chapter as well

Ved: Dont forget our love

Ved: Dont forget wat we mean

Ahmir: As i said..... I might come crawling back.... But for that to happen..... I need to first go

Ved: U r asking after all dis

Ahmir: I won't..... I can't

Ved: What kind a joke is this, man?

Ahmir: Remember we still have to flirt

Ved: This is no timepass

Ved: Ahmir stop it

Ved: U r telling me

Ved: I shld make peace to let u go

Ved: Seriously???????

Ved: This is no movie Ahmir u can choose how it will end ...

Ved: We need to watch our step

Ved: We need to think wisely

Ved: Man, a lot happens in a married life

Ved: And its us who said it ..

Ved: We will not let anyone go

Ved: We will stick no matter wat happend

Ved: Happens

Ahmir: We also said ... We will kill each other

Ved: Its ok

Ved: Its just not about relationship... its about coul to soul connections which is divine

Ved: I feel i just woke up

Ved: Our love is strong enough to deal with such negatives... lets make effort to fix it and not let it go

Ved: Lets not do this ... pls lets work towards fixing it.

Ved: Ahmir its nt am nt in my senses

Ved: Actually sm back in my senses

Ved: Am*

Ved: This adrenaline rush that we were going through ... about me myself....... dis isnt wat we r

Ahmir: Ved read what you are writing

Ved: Wat

Ahmir: This is madness...... I have made you mad.... This is nothing but shock... Denial.... Anger... Love... Sadness

Ved: Are you done writing....

Ahmir: It is bound to happen

Ved: Am very much in my senses Ahmir

Ved: Am trying to get u back in senses

Ved: Relationships don't work with logics and rules

Ahmir: I am in senses

Ahmir: Its me

Ved: Our love isnt abt just

Ved: Physically surrounding... Ahmir its soul spirit mind and body

Ved: This relationship had gods blessings its his gift

Ved: We r saying we wanna let it go .... why??? Coz i need space

Ved: Seriously ??? We are so stoned to let eachother go?? Really?? Are we so hungry for space?

Ahmir: No not space.... We need to find who we are

Ved: We knw who we r

Ved: This isnt a myserty

Ved: Its simple

Ahmir: And that's why we are where we are

Ved: N we can figure it out together

Ved: I dnt love u just fr ur good things

Ved: I love u wat is nt good per me

Ved: N dis isnt a dialgue

Ved: I mean it and my god knows it

Ahmir: I know that.... You love me.... But you want me in a certain way and you can't deny that

Ved: Ahmir

Ved: Every marriage relationship involved change

Ahmir: Will you be happy if i dont be what i am supposed to be

Ved: U r fyting wid me to let u go

Ahmir: I fought with me as well

Ahmir: And you saw it

Ved: U r nt fyting wid me to keep us together

Ved: Yes

Ved: Dnt fyt

Ahmir: I am no longer and that's why I am asking this

Ved: Ahmir these things i wanna be myself ... Such conversations happen in roadside relationships

Ahmir: Ved we are two individuals as well

Ved: Jin rishton mein rooh aur rohaani ki baaat ho... yeh sab petty hai

Ved: We r 2 individusls

Ahmir: Ved Stop it man

Ahmir: We have killed eachothers soul

Ved: We let our soul connect bfr we cld connect

Ved: Dat is nt true

Ved: U wanna say n run away

Ved: Bt dat isnt true

Ahmir: We love each other.... But as you said we don't like each other

Ved: Ahmir dnt latch onto smthing i said wen i knw i was doing stupidity

Ved: N taking high societal grounds

Ahmir: No social grounds Ved

Ahmir: Its me....

Ved: Den dnt tell me u love

Ved: Me etc etc

Ved: We r gonna damage ourselves more

Ved: N i can see dat

Ved: U dnt like it .... but we r nt from planet ... we r indian fsmilies ... we value family challenges sacrifices tough times

Ahmir: Ved at this point I am ready to take all the blame but not ready to make a mistake of what we have trying do to for last month almost

Ahmir: We have made each other miserable

Ved: Stop it

Ved: U r painting and disrepecting our love

Ved: As sm stench

Ahmir: I will take that blame too.

Ved: We havent become miserble ... No bomb blast happened

Ved: Am seriously nw angry at u... bt i love u fr dat too ...

Ved: Why

Ved: Coz my love n madness fr u

Ved: Is wayyyyyy higher

Ahmir: Be angry.... Its healthy

Ved: N all dis isnt smthing matters

Ahmir: I have beaten myself blue in past for it and i know it helps

Ved: U r pushing tooo hard to break away

Ved: I wont say breakfree

Ved: Nothing nothing .... nothing has happened which is permanent dent... its temp block dat happend

Ahmir: Then i beg you to let it test the time

Ved: If our love is strong all of dis seems way tooo smll

Ved: Arjun aur duryodhan ne kya maaanga tha.... mahabharat ka result wahi teh ho gaya tha....

Ved: Tabhi if u believe in krishna .... soch ke maaang .... i dnt think dis bet is worth to put our relationship on the table...

Ved: Dis spell on our relationship is on d nth moment .... u want to let go off me den say it out loud .... dnt put it to test ... phirrr isse bhi badi misery hogi n dere will be no turn back

Ved: We need to read d writing on d wall... dis isnt d time to loose the rope ....

Ved: Like its saiD humarey rishtey pe kaal bhaitha hai .... dekhna yeh hai kaun jitega

Ved: Ur comment on fridge

Ved: Had d power to hit me

Ved: N i have realized d meaning of it

Ved: Consequence of it

Ved: Dnt loose d rope Ahmir

Ved: Yeh galti karne ka mann nahi maan raha

Ved: Humne ek chhoti si apni duniya banayee hai .... dnt watch it crumble .... help me hold it n fix it

Ved: We can Figure all and evrtything out .... slowly and together ...

Ved: Agar gayee to phirr gayiii

Ved: I can see dat too

Ved: Matt kar yeh galti and dnt let me do it either baby

Ved: I can only beg now

Ved: I rest all my case Ahmir

Ved: In front of u

Ved: 🙏

Ahmir: Dont.... The message says it all on the fridge..... I am right there.... Just not visible.

Ved: Naaah u knw n i.knw ....

Ved: Matt kar yeh galti

Ahmir: If you have faith in our love..... Let it prove me wrong

Ved: Haaath se nikli naaav ... nadi mein sirf behti hai

Ved: Waaapis nahi aati

Ved: U let it go ... its nt cmng ... nt coz i dnt believe in our love ... i believe in time and time is a healer and it get d spell on u n makes u move on... our world doesnt deserve to be put to test ....

Ved: Its a small one .... let it be Ahmir .... we will fix it and if nothing live in it fr sure

Ved: Its nt dat bad ....

Ahmir: Who are we kidding.... We have come to this.... It is that bad

Ved: Its nt

Ahmir: We are here for a reason

Ved: If u think am nt one of d reasons den fly away and dnt tell me u r here for den we r truly kidding

Ved: Coz if i cldnt hold u nw i wont

Ved: Ever

Ved: If u still want to push our little nest out to break... i wont say anything further ...i wont be aaking si i didnt believe it

Ved: Believe in it

Ved: U knw me

Ahmir: Probably that's where I am being a jerk.... I am sand.... Hold me tight and i will slip away..... And i guess thats what i have been saying.... I have lost myself

Ved: Dnt be abtract relations arent....

Ved: U wanna slip

Ved: Do dat

Ved: U have lost urself and increasesd d space between us .... where we didnt talk to eachother

Ved: I guess u r more dan willing to push me away us away ....

Ved: D more i m pushing u r adding weight to ur persistence ....

Ved: Go ahead ... nw I see u

Ahmir: I will take that blame too....

Ved: Am memserized wid d passion wid which u pushing.... just wish it was fr us

Ved: And dnt take d blame

Ved: I have shown my paagalpanti

Ved: U r showing

Ved: Its d cause bt madness to acheive d cause dats wanting to win

Ved: Its nt*

Ved: I love u Ahmir

Ved: And i rest my case soul and heart here .... in true sense ... no more push .... god will help u

Ved: Learn wat i meant

Ved: Muaaaah

Ved: U r a free bird if u want to

Ved: N i love u

Ahmir: I know......

Ahmir: And let me be the jerk you think I am

Ved: Am nt thinking anything Ahmir

Ved: Now he is up smiling fr he knws wat i meant

Ahmir: I love you too..... I know its not believable right now.... And i will have him punish me for what I have done to you.... To us and to everyone involved.

Ved: No punishment baby .... i still cant see u in pain...

Ved: I was helping u in smthin i believe u needed

Ved: I want him to bless u wid everything

Ved: I was giving u my everything

Ved: Fr my love like i have said in d past ... allah ko bhi shikwa hai ... mere pyaaar se ... woh bhi ziddi koshish kar raha ....

Ved: Mazaaa to yeh hai usme bhi aaapki khushi hai... aur aapki khushi mein hi meri khushi hai

Ved: I also pray fr d core of my heart u find smone .... kyunki main bhi toh dekhu kisski himmat hai .... meri ibaadat ko byaaan karne mein

Ved: 🌹 Tumne mera pyaaar ki hadd nahi dekhi .... intezaaar kar. Main chup rahunga.. wahi allah uske geet gayega.

"TEMPTATIONS ARE FATAL... DON'T TRY THEM AT HOME"

"IF THERE ARE MANY REASONS TO QUIT BUT ONE TO HOLD ON... HOLD ONTO TO THAT ONE REASON"

The Yellow Silence

Having you around, your yellow shirt brightens my day

Your smile makes me feel nice

I make conscious effort to look into your eyes

Only to hear you say ... Hello How are you?

You stare at me everytime I pass by... For I feel you

Your cute smile and your warm hands

I desire to feel them hence I desire to hold

I know you are not mine

And truly i dont want it either

But your gaze makes me want you

I remember when you tried talking about some other guy on the TV

I took that chance to tease you with it like a breezy

You smile and laugh and smirked at me

It made me tease you more

Tease you like i didn't want to let you go

You blushed you laughed out loud

I knew nothing is brewing but i knew i wanted to see tinkling eyes

And innocent smile... looking for an-escape route

For my unedited teasing around

I remember when I see you leaving,

I feel a breathe of Fresh air walking out

There is nothing that can happen for you wanna come clean

And I just want to see you to feel the Fresh air within

So keep walking in everyday... Keep asking me

As to how I feel everyday for it does make me feel Good

It does make me feel nice about myself

It does push me to look at you and feel I can trigger different norms.

If only i could help you let loose

I Will drag you down the road

Look into your drunkard eyes

And dance with you all over

Feel your beard tinkling mine

Coming close to your lips

Without letting it shine

Untill that happens ... which is almost not gonna be the case

I will continue to look for everyday you deep intence gaze

DONT LIMIT THE THOUGHT PROCESS OF A CHILD... IT MAY BE A FIRE OF A NEW INNOVATION!!!

Life full of chaos... harmony danger, possibilities and whatever you make out of it!!!
- Sarovar Ghissing

RESPECT HER!!! SHE IS BEAUTIFUL ... NO MATTER WHAT'S HER SHAPE COLOR SIZE IS!!
– Puneet Pandey

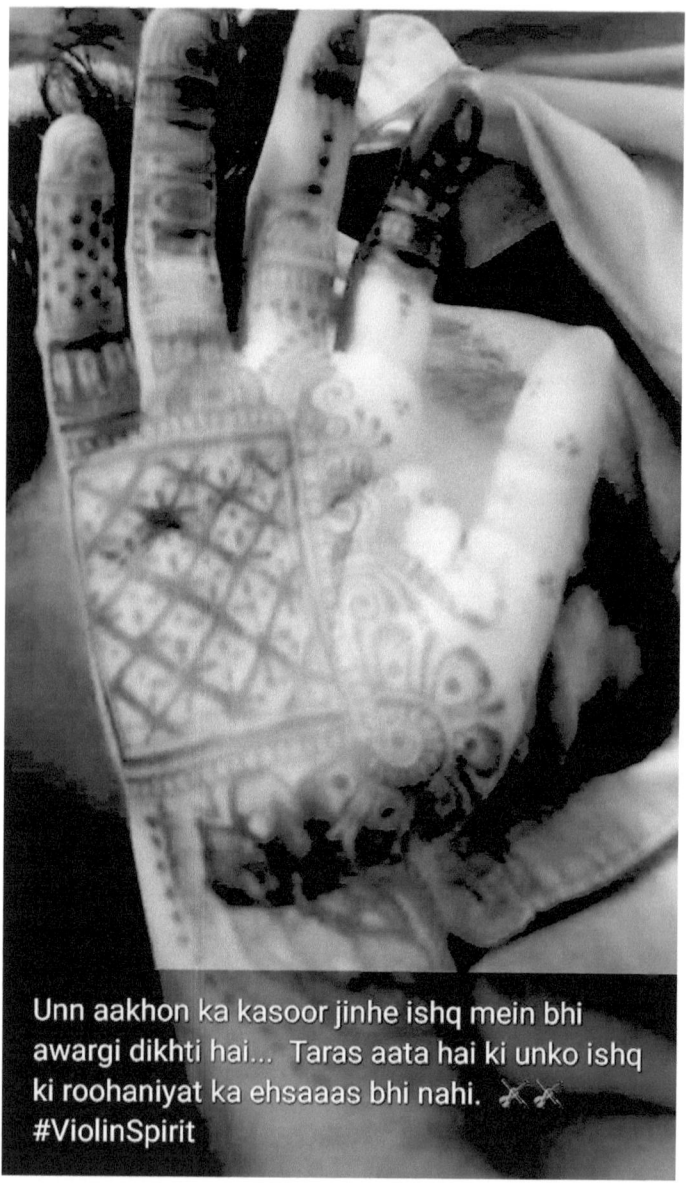

Leh'd On My Birthday

I was in the middle of nowhere when I decided to travel to Leh. It was something I needed to do as a ritual for my birthday … But this time it was different… it was alone … My solo trip… It was exactly 3 months since we both separated … a mistake I think made in haste …. I was looking through the travel dates and I realized it will be that time of the day when there is hardly anyone.

Those tears wrenched eyes … Those crying out loud in the middle of the night… Those moments to hurt myself with iron… I guess things became very unsettled and I was making conscious effort to remain intact at work. And I didn't want to be alone at home for my birthday … and I couldn't think of any other place than Leh for it would make me be peace … and maybe somewhere closer to him.

Nov 28th and I decided to book the tickets a week before. I needed to pack everything for this time it was going to be just me and I needed to take care of myself more than ever… coz there wasn't anyone to remind me to pack important stuff… look for right place to stay in … My mind was very vulnerable and very unsure if it was a right decision… The decision to go to the place where he and I had formed great memories and the best time of my life… I knew I needed to find a place where there was silence peace and the stars… Leh was it.

I was done packing and ready to leave for the airport when I realized I couldn't find my keys. I began panicking and knew I had no time to waste. I was all over… The lights were off so I was sweating and didn't have the mind to turn them on. The taxi driver was waiting for me to board and I couldn't find the key. The flight was at 6:30am and it was 4:00am already. I closed my eyes and told god " Please help me find the keys and I will give INR 100/-". Every passing minute was building up and making me more anxious.

What would be my alternative? I didn't want to bother him with my madness but if nothing, I thought I will ask him to lock the gate with the keys, a set that he had...maybe a hope but he had told that he doesn't want anyone to dictate his life.... I couldn't believe he had built so much anger for me.... Even after me leaving but I guess I knew he wasn't fighting with me but within.

Finally, I found my keys kept underneath the clothes. I ran like wind to lock the gate and boarded the taxi.

It was 5:00am when I reached airport and boarded the plane by 6:30am ready to leave... I wasn't too keen to have free time ... And I saw a text from him "Enjoy the flight and do have a coffee." My mind sank .... I was crying out loud within for I felt motionless...aimless and directionless... For a moment I thought of boarding a different plane... I guess I was fighting within and knew nothing ... who would win.... Or if at all anyone would win.

The heart was beating fast for I didn't know what to expect and how to manage everything ... Then I realized that this is how things are going to be and hence I need to take control of things ... I saw the list of flights on the display board to tell me my options to escape; and I chose to get LEH'D.

The flight was fully packed.

It had monks, army men and a lot of other people. I could see people excited, but I had no clue why I was feeling I was amidst no man's land.... You hate it when you wanna be with the one ... but the one doesn't wanna be with you. Singlehood is painful ...

Weigh the options and see how it can be daunting. Lived as live-in .... When your day begins and ends with the person...

seeing and fighting... Taking pot shots at eachother and yet cuddle up on the bed... we were the perfectly imperfect.... I wondered if it was about the people, we were surrounded with ... And finding a sense of assurance of the norm of dumping ... I couldn't conclude.... It didn't seem like what it was.

I looked around, quickly kept my luggage in the cabin and began looking for my seat. I sat on my seat and saw a couple sitting and waiting to begin their first honeymoon. Suddenly I remembered the first time we were going to Leh and the excitement he had on his face made me love him more.

I was excited then for it was our first trip far away. He insisted to sit on the window seat and relinquished after my face insisting otherwise.

I sat on the seat and closed my eyes. The heart was pounding for the unknown ... yet I knew that I would be able to manage things... especially when I could manage the local trains in Mumbai... this seemed a cakewalk. Really??!! Naah... To tell you the truth, it wasn't something I had experienced ever and I pray nobody does. Not even during my first.

The couple began clicking the pics and recording the video the moment we flew, and I remembered how he insisted to record the take off video. I began listening to music and closed my eyes... No music and no noise would make me think of things I was trying to not let impact me.

Suddenly, I remembered when he held me last time and kissed me on my forehead and held my hand to the door to let go.

The moment still gave me pain for I regretted letting him do things per his whims. I still remembered how it would have been great to have him around and create more memories, but I guess it wasn't meant to be this way.

I had had my personal trust issues with my first relationship wherein my ex treated me like a non-serious affair and tried hooking me with someone else. I still remember my ex two-timing me and trying to hook me up with one of his friends. All this combined with my fear of him cheating me for I wasn't living upto the expectations.

And suddenly I heard the announcement of some turbulence. There was enough within already…. The turbulence wasn't an easy ….. nothing like in the past … The seats were literally moving, and I began praying …thinking that it was time to say Hasta La Vista but as Single?? NO!!!

Fortuanetly, everything got normal few minutes later. Nothing of the sort happened and we landed very smoothly.

I was all set with my scarf and long coat… prepared to land at the land of -9* degrees … It was freezing cold yet the sunlight was hitting the eyes. Imagine landing in the middle of the mountains … freezing and clear sky. I just wished I could fly and not land at all.

I tried getting my luggage. As usual I was over packed, and I had 4 bags. I was ready for all eventualities. It was a tough moment for I had to carry all 4 bags and manage things on my own unlike last times when he would guide me through.

I felt angry at that moment for feeling helpless and then I reminded myself that there wasn't any other alternative and I needed to buckle up.

I carried my luggage directly to the small store that sold Tea and Maggie and his favorite omelet. I had the customary tea and left to look for a taxi. Luckily, I saw a taxi waiting outside.

Usually its hard to find a taxi during this weather and I knew that I need not bargain and just board. But the driver was kinder and charged me INR150 to drop me at the venue; The challenge was I didn't know the place for I hadn't booked my hotel and needed to do some hunting.

But I decided to explore the same hotel that he booked last time. I tried searching for it and landed at the same hotel. The hotel offered a traditional stoll and I hoarded 2 more. I asked for the availability and the receptionist shared the price and I was shocked.

I pretended I knew they were overcharging and mentioned that the price they charged last time was half the price at that moment. I didn't expect her to put in effort in investigating. She asked me about the dates and the name for registration. She looked into the computer and denied any such booking. I insisted, and they referred his number to locate the booking.

I was hoping that my bluff will be helpful when suddenly she printed the booking and handed over to me. I couldn't believe it was indeed 3 times more than I was bargaining for; But what did strike me was the booking under Mr and Mrs. Sharma.

I had my emotions running high. I snapped out and told myself to focus on the issue at hand. I wasn't going to put in that kind of money for a room; hence I decided not to go with that hotel but rather explore other places and asked the driver to help in finding a budget hotel.

He took me to a hotel. It was a decent and within my budget. I took the room and went off to sleep to rest immediately.

Later, I woke up to go to the market closeby. Leh has a usual mall road but it was clean less crowded and active.

I knew I had to be back to the hotel early, but I still wanted to visit different places closeby, so I hired a taxi to take me to Sangam.

Sangam is a beautiful place and I was the only one present there. It was serene and beautiful. There was no one to click photographs for usually he used to click me, and I was the model. I wrote his name using the stones on the sand and screamed his name for one could hear the echo.

I asked the driver to help me with the photography and he was super excited to do the job. We clicked a selfie too and he was all smiles.

I came back to the market and asked him to help me plan my trip to Pangong lake and Khardungla Pass. He asked for INR15K and I knew it was over quoted and beyond my budget, so I didn't pursue much.

Walking on the street, I began searching for the same hotel where we ate Chinese last time. I didn't want to eat Chinese though, but I guess memory lane was driving me... anyways I opted for a Punjabi restaurant. I know it may be weird to many, but I was very hungry and didn't want to play with my taste buds. When I ordered the food, I realized I didn't have the cash for he used to usually manage the finances, so I ran to withdraw cash. It was exactly a year when I remember I was talking to Tiara about how her boyfriend cheated on her and appeared non regretful and I was consoling her while he was around me.

Tiara's boyfriend and he were good friends and I always insisted that her boyfriend wasn't serious. It was a roller coaster for me. I looked at the café and thought of the time when I was debating with him about the same thing and for the first time, he agreed with me. I missed being taken care off, being pampered and shouted at for doing my drama.

I knew I was building a guilt within for not stopping him .. but the most regretful was when he asked me if we should go for a trip to save us and not part ways .... and I didn't push much on it ... Maybe it would have saved ... I guess I was weak then .

Even at the moment, I regret feeding him with thoughts about larger than life and how 'cool' it will be …. I can never forgive myself for falling for the trap of being larger than life and idealistic. I guess it doesn't work and it shouldn't be… I knew I had my fare share of making him feel the way he felt about himself … unknowingly I was proving the stories in his mind as the truth when it was all farce… I trusted him more than myself … I just feared being push to a situation when I am confronted with that situation…. I knew he was more than important he thought was … but I guess I didn't acknowledge that …. I knew I didn't let him have the feeling that he spends more for I used to pro actively try to pay for things… It wasn't like I didn't want him to pay but I just wanted him to save money for mom dad and himself and he was already bearing the cost of being my partner…

I guess I thought it's the same money and I could spend mine and use his when really needed… I guess I failed in making that point clear…. He always wanted to be the one in control and I liked that … I knew I was miserable in that … but something changed, and he withdrew from that ownership.

I came back to the restaurant and my food was ready…

It was yummy; imagine all the spices and green chillies and tawa roti. The aroma and the ambiance… Life is all about about that. It had different spices and I felt like heaven with the first bite. I had my first bite and I moaned loudly as a feeling of sigh. I ate it quickly for it was dark already, paid the bill and came back home.

The roads were darker, and I knew I needed to run before some wild animal or someone attacked me. Though, people in Leh are extremely hospitable and kind.

I still remember we had met with an accident the previous time and the driver damaged his car and his teeth, but the driver still came to our hotel to check on us.

It was 11 kms away from the place where we had the accident. Someone was passing by and he dropped us back to the hotel. Kind people and honest human beings!!!

I just knew I was safe yet the darkness was louder.

I realized what mesmerized me when we met with the accident last time; The stars The sky. I simply couldn't take my eyes off. It was clear and shinning with billion stars. My desires to fly in space got its fuel and I was very excited to keep looking at the sky when the hotel came. I had a sense of relief and waited in the open balcony.

My brother in law called me asking me to share the name of my hotel and whereabouts in case of emergency and I reluctantly gave the information. I knew they all would have been worried for they knew about my separation and I was far off alone.

I had a cup of tea and entered my room. It was 11:50pm and somebody knocked my door. I was a little skeptical for it was too late for any room service and I hadn't asked for anything until it could have been my sister who could have called the hotel to check on me.. Maybe my phone wasn't reachable.

I still remember the day when I was at work and my phone had died and she came to my office with her newly born kid and her husband. I was so mad at her then and felt guilty as well.

I checked my phone to see if there were missed calls but there were none. I opened the door and had the shock of my life!

My brother in law was there standing right in front of me with the cake and began singing birthday wishes for it was midnight and my birthday!

I was taken aback and clueless. He hugged me and asked me to cut the cake.

I was still digesting the fact that my brother in law traveled so far to be with me.. Was it my sister's idea or his idea? I just didn't know what to make of it.

And while I was about the cut the cake, my phone rang and he called to wish me. My whole body was smiling in happiness ... he had texted as well, and it meant a lot to me, but I knew he wasn't coming back.

I told him that my brother in law had given a surprise and I felt it didn't sink well with him... Maybe he was feeling the same as I was.

I celebrated my birthday.... not alone as planned; I was curious as to how did he plan all this and how did he get the cake arranged. I couldn't stop asking him questions.

I was happy yet unsettling for I didn't want to celebrate my birthday. I decided to respect my brother in law's effort and emotions.

My sister video chatted with me to wish me and talk about the surprise. And he began asking me questions about my plan for the rest of the day. I appeared clueless but decided to play along. We decided that we will tour the nearest spots in the city and then see how the rest plays out.

Next day, after touring the city, I came back to the hotel and slept over. The hotel had guests celebrating their anniversaries and birthday on the same day and I was sleeping.

Suddenly someone knocked the door. I woke up and was irritated for I was tired and had bad headache.

A drunk man entered my room asking me to come down and celebrate instead of sleeping. I insisted to remain in the room and that he should leave. He looked at me and tried removing my quilt to drag me out. I looked at him angrily and told him to shove off.

My brother in law screamed asking me to come out. I went out and saw my brother in law dancing and drunk. He insisted that I should come down and celebrate; I was adamant to be allowed to have my time and space for I wasn't in the mood.

Suddenly the same man popped up and held my hand to drag me out.

I shouted and told him "What the F#$% is this? Go away" he persisted and came closer to me. I pushed him away and told him to mind his business instead of trying to pretend.

My brother in law screamed from the ground floor for he was drunk and dancing with the inmates and told me to come down for a photo.

I went down when another drunk man held me trying to kiss me. I turned and looked into his eyes angrily and walked out. That guy came running towards the stairs and held my hand. I threw my hand in air and shouted "Dare you hold my hand and do this again. I don't want to spoil the mood so if you want to continue enjoy the party, leave NOW!!! ". The guy was taken aback, and he left.

I felt out of place and insecure. I thought of calling him, but his mother had told me that he was out for a party and that he couldn't have answered my phone. I was very unsettled and felt violated. I called a friend, who was around him, to check on him and tell him.

I didn't receive any call back. I tried reaching out to another friend when he told me that he had gone out with some new guy hanging around.

I was not happy for I really needed a sense of security and I couldn't have discussed it with my family; It wasn't about the new guy but about the fact that I was so dependent on him emotionally; Never had that happened ...I thought I just needed to let go and should be going off to sleep when I saw a missed call from him.

I called him back and told him about what happened and how I felt. His response seemed logical but sin any emotion. I realized its not same anymore and I decided to let go off the conversation.

That night I realized what was happening in life.... Life will throw you ruthlessly and you just ought to pick up from there.

I hope you can imagine what I must have gone through..... You are alone and lonely... The worst reality to realize!!

I called my sister and shouted at her. She shared her inability to manage my brother in law's drinking issues. I decided to sleep over it for I knew my brother in law had experienced a lot of emotional ups and downs and he must be wanting to celebrate.

I went off to sleep and woke up with the anticipated headache. All the plans for the day were canceled and my brother in law didn't push me either. I guess it was also about me rebelling against everything around.

The next day we needed to visit Pangong lake and I was super excited for that was a moment I wish I could freeze.

If you have seen the lake, you would know what I mean. Life stops... the world isn't the same anymore and you become a person unsure off.

I realized that this was my brother in law's first trip to Leh and I became his unofficial guide. I realized that I needed to respect my brother in law's effort to visit me for he didn't really need to do all.

We boarded the taxi and began our journey. The roads were breath taking... The pheran that I was wearing made me look like a locality. I knew I just wanted to immerse myself in the winds, the air and the life around Leh.

The journey and scenic sight were growing on me... from ice capped mountains to dry sand hills... To narrow lanes and rocky roads to clean wide roads.... I still can recollect the passage where the ice must me 3 ft and imagine what would you want to do ... We got down multiple times to play with ice on the road. Imagine white sheet of ice and scorching sun.

Nature is the most powerful and beautiful and I felt so shallow to even think of letting life pass through the emotions.... Have you ever thought of the fact that life existed before humans and will exists before us? Have you ever imagined that we are simply a dot in the universe; I felt so small ... more so with the thought that we may be so big in the world ... All I saw reminded me of how every second we let go is a second we leave for history... I know I wouldn't get a chance to live that second again yet we get embroiled in emotions.... I just wished I could really embrace it all.... And by the time I could snap out of my world, we had reached the lake.

Huge mountains covered with snow… The freezing breeze and the blue water…. The sound of the water really talking to you …. And you don't see a life beyond yourself!!!

I just wanted to live as much that moment with my eyes as possible…. I don't think I can ever do justice what it does and did to me …. I cried like a child … more to do with the fact that how misplaced our lives are and how much I am losing by being amidst the chaos… Not sure of anyone else but you feel trapped as a person and soul. This is one moment when I felt caged in open world back in the city for you are really not free… The nature didn't want us to be like that, but we have made it like that …. And that's why the birds are lucky…. I just wish I could turn into a bird and fly and not come back for I don't think that's what this life was meant to be.

My brother in law saw me crying … He didn't ask … I cried like a child, but I was freezing like snow too… My hands were cold, my hair was in the air and my eyes were filled with the sight of the what I saw. After a moment, I knew I needed to snap out for I wasn't going to stay for long and needed to be happy for what I was experiencing and seeing. I think my soul found its nest for some time.

We decided to explore the place in our taxi, and I sat on the window while the car was on and began moving to the tunes of the song that he and I shared as a soul song.

My mind needed peace and silence and the place offered more than that. We sat there and roamed around; Clicked pictures to capture every moment and breath.

We played music and danced like we cared little. It was just 3 of us; me the driver and my brother in law.

We just didn't want to go anywhere but instead just watch the slow water movements.

We went close to the lake and it wasn't frozen enough. The water was talking to us with great amusement. I don't think anyone can explain how one would feel. I was in a zone unknown and didn't want to move. I wanted to drink the water of the lake but presumingly it was salty and unfit for drinking… I wanted to jump on it… I wanted to share every moment and record it in my eyes.

I knew I was going to leave in about some more minutes, but I felt I was where I truly desire to belong to. All the pains, fears and vulnerability were not in my mind. The sky was embracing me with its arms… the mountains gave me safety and water my friend. I just didn't believe what I was going through at that moment.

I guess if you see it you will know. I know he liked mountains too and how much like a child he was dancing when we were here last. I missed him not just because he wasn't around but because I knew we are connected with the nature just same yet we were very different people. I wanted to take up the road walking to just feel and capture the moment until I return as a solace.

It was getting late enough and my brother in law was freezing. The breeze began talking and I was all over.

So, we decided to board and look for a store for a nice hot tea. We couldn't find one so we decided to just go back to the hotel.

We reached the hotel, ate some food and went off to sleep ... a much deserving one and a fulfilling.

We needed to be ready for the next day travel to Khardungla pass. And I was super excited.

Next day, I woke up early to get ready and move for the taxi. In 30 minutes, we were ready for the moment.

We boarded the taxi and moved further. The driver told us that the snow is about 7 ft for last night, there was heavy snowfall.

I was on top of the 'mountain' to know that the snowfall had us 7 feet road covered. We were excited to move to reach the venue and the journey was mesmerizing.... Imagine you are in the middle of nowhere and you just see snow. You could feel the coldness by the breathing.

I was very enthralled to see my brother in law with him wanting to click pics. I was I guess at a moment overwhelmed with his over the top desire to do everything for the social media, but I realized his desire to feel nice and relaxed.

I must admit that the desire to be desired and affirmations isn't a good sign of a balanced mind but some realities can't be debated.

When I reached there, I could see myself sitting at the corner of the road and him clicking me. I clicked better pictures of him than he did but I knew I was very excited to walk farther than I did previous time.

So, I walked ahead to go through the road and see mountains far away and hearing my voice echoing ... I wish I could stop the moment and just freeze like the snow.

Luckily, we found a tea store opened unlike last time and I had 3 cups of tea. We had great time and were excited to return.

I think I left my heart at Pangong lake and I just wished I hadn't done stupid things. I was overwhelmed with the love I got from the mountains, lake and silence.

I felt I was back... I felt I was meant to be here... I felt I needed to realize that the worldly desires makes you not see what the world has to offer.

I remember I ran far onto the road with the belief that my world is changing. I might not be the same anymore... I wasn't meant to be I guess.

Unwillingly, we decided to return and I wasn't ready to bid adieu to the real life.

But realities are the cuffs that help us value these possibilities.

We returned home and I went off to sleep to wake up for dinner.

When I woke up, I wasn't really hungry for food; It was the hunger for the soul.

I saw the mountains from the balcony and my tears trickled ... and it wasn't about him. It was about my dreams to be in the sky amongst the stars and I was literally seeing each of them talking to me.

It was 9pm when my brother in law called me to eat. I didn't realize but my brother in law was overwhelmed as well.

I looked at him and asked if he wanted to share or talk about. I knew he was holding up something very deep and when he did share his secret about his childhood, I was stunned yet I felt for the kid who had to go through all that he did.

I saw the man of his past and the man who made some decisions due to that and that emotions ran in his mind very strongly.

Nothing in life is temporary

Yet nothing is permanent either

Our lives are entangled with a lot of people

Our desires are our hooks that keep us away

I may not desire everything that is good for me

I do care about how my life unfolds

Every-time I look at sky… I look at the moon and

I tell myself

Someday I will hope to be there on the moon or sky

Someday if not in person but maybe in form of love for someone

Someday I will know what I truly deserve and what I really want

And that day I will hopefully decide to hold that tight enough

Tight enough not to let it slip like sand but tight enough

To know it will always remain in my hand … in his hands…

We silently went off to sleep with a mind overwhelmed with the emotions.

We woke up the next day and got ready to return. His flight was early, but we decided to walk and leave together. The hotel was kind enough to drop us to the airport.

My brother in law hugged me before leaving. He had come to be my shoulder for the night only to realize that he needed a shoulder himself to figure out life as it turned out to be than the life he wanted it to be. In few minutes, he was off to his plane.

I was waiting for my flight when I stepped out and looked around. I held a stone and threw in the air ... The desire to touch the sky and stars without seeing the stone falling... Keeping my promise that I might shall return and steal these moments from my life for myself and no one else to have anything to say... The desire to live with the belief that the dream to touch the sky isn't really a bad idea ... only if I dared to ...

It was my flight time and I boarded the plane. Tears were flowing for I was leaving behind or carrying it along with me.

As soon as I landed and reached home, I saw a big painting and a letter from him... The painting had the photographs of me ,framed, of my trips with him .. The frame looked empty though it had me all over; it was him who was missing.

My feet were shaking and like a mad man I ran to meet him and celebrate my birthday; I bought a cake and the gifts that I got for the family. When I reached his place, I got to know that he was sleeping so I returned. I opened the letter to read it again and it said

"LIFE HAS TO OFFER YOU MORE .. LET IT SERVE"

"TRUE LOVE IS A RARE PHENOMENON … INDULGE IN IT"

Mars Was Always On The List

I had reached the airport to travel to Chennai. I wasn't sure if I was ready for a long trip, but I knew I wanted it as much.

It was 6:00am when I landed at the airport when my sister called to check on me. Carol was always worried about my whereabouts for her single brother staying alone terrified her as much.

After my goodbyes, I was very impatiently waiting for the journey to begin. I was waiting for the flight announcements when the ground staff announced change in my boarding gate. I knew I had very less time, so I ran towards the door. I knew I didn't want to miss the flight and that the flight operations would be mindful of the time gap to reach the opposite side of the airport.

But finally! I reached and boarded the plane.

The plane was full of people and I felt claustrophobic. I decided to return to my seat and closed my eyes for I hadn't had sleep for last few days.

The plane was ready to take off and the woman sitting next to me asked me questions about my plans. Then, she asked me for where I planned to get down. Get Down??!!!

It was a strange question for her to ask for the flight was destined to go to Chennai. I jokingly said ... "Well! its going to Mars and I will drop you at the moon."

She smiled and turned her face.

"Who asks such questions in a flight that was meant to reach a direct destination." I thought trying to convince myself of not being out of civic sense in responding the way I did.

And I went off to the sleep after listening to the usual aircraft announcements. My eyes were burning, and I turned my mind off from everything at work.

I asked myself to detoxify my mind and sleep.

Few hours later, I opened my eyes and I couldn't believe where I was.

I looked around and I could only see red sand and mountains out of the window and the seat looked very unusual.

I looked at the back and it just had nothing except my luggage. I couldn't believe myself for it looked like a space ship and the announcement said "This is your destination from moon and that I needed to get down or else the space craft will fly back."

"Spacecraft!!!???"

I panicked and didn't know what to do. I didn't know what was happening for I was somewhere I wasn't supposed to be. I knew I didn't have much time to decide and I went off to the backseat to see where was I. When I moved out of the craft, it was written MarsOrbitorMission10. I couldn't believe what was I reading. Suddenly I realized I had a helmet on and the oxygen cylinder. I didn't know what to do.

This was unreal.... Scary and haunting!!!

If I had boarded the craft and moved forward, I may have had no chance of reaching safely and if I had stayed at the red zone, I knew I wouldn't have survived longer.

I tried checking my 'craft' to see that there were enough supplies for me ... but enough for what?

I didn't even know what was happening. I felt like I was in a dream. I tried slapping myself to know if it was for real or a dream. It turned out that I can slap really hard and it was painful.

Reality bit me and I realized some how I had reached Mars…

Just like what I told the woman.

Who was that woman? And why would this happen to me? I don't even know how to operate the craft. I knew I was f#$%%ed!!!

I got all my supplies down when the final warning told that the craft will fly anyways.

I thought I needed to keep the craft for future and decided to turn off the navigation system and the whole setup. And it did work!!!

I was in some deep crap. "How could I be so far and in a plane?" "Why did I say what I said to the woman?" "If only I knew this would happen, I would have said some other planet that may host a life or a different country. Not a no mainland or rather no life land."

I thought it must be some magic or something and waited for the magic to end. But hours later I realized this wasn't a joke. It was literally happening. I was at Mars ... alone and with my only aircraft that I never knew how to fly.

Somehow the supplies were way more, and I didn't know how to react. My mind seemed choked and throat frozen.... Or may be the opposite ... I didn't know what was happening to me. I couldn't cry for I didn't want to waste the oxygen but then I thought "I am not going to survive this is truth. The witch had gotten me here and I have nowhere to go. Why would this happen to me?"

I was full of questions and my body was holding onto its weight. I cried and cried thinking of people who would be waiting for me. I was totally dead... if that could happen on Mars. I boarded the plane and sleptover like I didn't care, or I was giving up with the idea of surviving this spell or whatever it was.

I guess I went off to sleep to try if all of that was farce and could be reversed.

After some time, I opened my eyes and I was still at the place that I was. The red sand place!

Now I knew I wasn't going back and that I was meant to be there. If I was there with the way I had reached, there would be a purpose and I was very unsure of what that purpose looked like.

I tried opening the shelves in the craft to see if it had some notes or books to refer to. I opened the door of the craft and jumped on the land. I was feeling very light and needed to find some food to eat. I didn't know if I was going to find something vegetarian... I smiled at myself ... as a fool for food was a luxury and not as a need at that moment. My body was active but my mind needed food to digest.

I opened my supplies bag and it had water bottles and some packed food items to munch. I was up for a mind messing moment. I needed my tea ... my milk... my books and phone....

"Oh my god where and why the hell I am in this situation? What did I do wrong? I have been nice to everyone and I didn't deserve this!!! My mother must be worried .. what will happen to her? What about my family? They would be stressed. They would be in terrible shape." God damn, why am I here." I kept talking to myself for I still couldn't believe I was where I was.

I needed to see someone to know and confirm where was I. The name on the craft meant I was on Mars. I was simply in awful state and couldn't come to terms that I was in a place unknown.

"Is it really a different planet or a set up or is it a different country that looks like Mars? But the announcement said ...

moon... no way I am going to moon.... But isn't that closer to earth. But I saw a series that spoke of aliens on Moon and that they killed people. But I had heard of aliens on Mars too. And I didn't know if any of that was true. And what if it was true? Was I amongst an unknown species?? Well of everything I can think off, I knew I was bound to die...hook or by another crook on the planet." My mind was as messed up as my life. I could only see red sand and brown sky.

Winds were blowing too loudly and strong. I had nowhere to hide except the craft. And I didn't have anything to check my time on.

My phone wasn't working, and I regretted not having a watch.

Since childhood, I hated wearing a watch. I used to feel trapped with anything around my wrist. And imagine, I was literally trapped in an unknown land. ... not just a land but a planet. Well I began to walk around to see what was around and I only could see huge mountain like structures but nothing else.

I had to bite the bullet .... Like literally I thought of killing myself instead of having to go through all that. I was numb and clueless about when would all of that would end. And it seemed it wasn't going to end at all.

I thought of walking towards the weird mountains ... The sky literally had the sun shinning yet I felt lighter for I know that the gravity at Mars wasn't strong as much as Earth.

Suddenly I saw something weird and that was a moving satellite orbiting the Mars... It was weird... right? How would anyone know??? How can a satellite be so visible, and then, I saw the moon...? Not the earth moon it was little shady like an asteroid and I missed seeing my moon... the moon at the earth ...cute little shinning object. The surface was rocky, yet I could see very unimpressed cuttings ... due to natural wind phenomenon, I guess.

I was very unhappy for I realized that this is going to be my future... whatever little was left. I tried walking towards a mountain, and something struck me... It had a something which could look like a pillar .... It was a very strange structure of mountains which was tall and yet cut into a very sharp pillar.... I was very surprised to see that for it signified some life settlement.... And I looked at the sky to see if I could see the earth.

But I couldn't see anything except a moon and a very strange Light.

I had no clue about night and day. I just lied on the way to close my eyes .... I heard the breeze and movement of winds and that was it... nothing... it was all as if I was in a dead place and there was no one else to rescue.

Transmitted-me pushed myself to go back to the craft and see what supplies I had and if I could read any paper in the craft. When I turned back, I realized I had walked a lot and all of it was quite far. I wasn't too keen to walk for so long so I decided to sit and relax for some more time and walk later.

I knew I needed to keep my body fitter but at the moment, the clueless me thought of resting.

When I woke up, I saw it was very bright and I realized that it was a morning for the sun was shinning. I thought of going back to the craft and seeing if I had any clothes to change or wear .... I couldn't track time for it wasn't easy to walk and I knew it would take longer... I came back and decided to see my supplies.

I needed to poop so I thought I will pick up a place to poop and let it be on the land for it to become fertile if not anything else. But it couldn't have been closer to the craft or supplies so then I decided to move towards the same place, and I noticed a crater kind towards the left.

I thought of using that as a place to 'store' my poop and pour some-water to test and see what might happen. I came back from the crater and looked for some clothes. There weren't any as expected, and I had no choice but to survive on what I had. I decided to clean the area around the craft to rest and I lied down.

My eyes were hurting again and were burning. I thought of sleeping and I closed my eyes.

When I opened my eyes, I saw the woman with her hand on my forehead and the passengers around. I just couldn't believe what I just saw ... The woman looked at me and said "Relax, what you are seeing is true but what you saw was true as well". I didn't know if I should trust her, but it felt real. I could see sand on my clothes. I asked the woman as to what did all this mean? She responded "Violin, you were in the midst of a realm experience wherein you were desired to be at different places, and you called out Mars. Remember there are different moments in life where it can define us. If you hadn't woken up before the flight, I would have had to leave you where you were and leave. The power of universe desired you to experience what you thought off."

I didn't know if it made any sense to me. I was mind messed for the fears came back. We came out of the plane and I wanted to run away from the woman. She looked at me and smiled "Don't worry you will see it again." And she left.

I was scared of what that meant. I ran to look for taxi and asked the driver to drop me at the house. I opened the door and came in when suddenly the lights went off. I was scared as hell and began praying, I sat near the chair and didn't move.

I wasn't sure if I should close my eyes... But I was tired, so I did.... I opened my eyes and the lights were on. I took a deep breath.

Next day I had to visit a friend, so I decided to book a taxi. The taxi came after 15 minutes and it began raining. One of my friend's friend had come-over and he wanted to discuss about some artifacts that were discovered and how he could get my help to put up in a famous museum. I asked if he would want to come-over and have some drinks while we discussed this project. He came-over and in no less time, we were on the bed.

Hours later, he spoke about the project and showed me the artifacts that they had discovered. And I was shocked to see the same pillar, edged out finely, there.

I was scared and he noticed it as well and responded "Something seems odd for you in these pics" I said nothing except this pillar. He told me that the pillar was excavated from a site near Harappa and that they wanted to get it to museum for it had drawing of some other planets. I didn't recall seeing any painting so I asked if I could see 360-degree pics of the pillar. When I turned the photos, I realized that it was exactly the same pillar, but I just missed seeing it the other side that moment when I was on 'mars'!!!??!

I needed answers and only the same woman could have given me the answers. I tried looking for the information about her, but nothing stood out. I decided to confide in a friend about this whole episode. My friend looked at me strangely ... like I had cracked the worst joke of the millennium or had a pot. I begged him to trust me, but he didn't. He tagged me as an insane wannabe and that I should focus on my life instead of trying to solve quantum physics etc.

I didn't know if anyone else would trust me so I asked my sister. The worried woman feared more now. She told me to avoid this and that. Nothing seemed logically or right. I didn't understand why did I see what I did.

Days later, I heard the news that a lander was seen on mars and that some foot steps were observed along with what they called human substance found on a crater.

All the space agencies were asked to declassify their files to ensure that no secret mission was conducted and if we had terraformed the planet. So if I could put it together, I was truly at Mars and that woman knew more than she let out.

I knew she would have heard about the news and would try and do something. But her smirk made me believe she wouldn't but rather let the world figure it out.

I was shocked and my friend who decided not to believe me came running to ask me if I was the guy on mars. I decided to underplay and joked "So you really did fall for what I said!! I knew it always!!! "

He bought the joke, but I wasn't too convinced myself. I knew something was bound to happen and I was waiting for it to unfold.

I sat on the sofa and began watching news. I felt asleep and I saw the woman walking towards me and telling me that I need to be prepared for the follow up expedition and I was very shivery.

She only answered my questions with a sentence "You were there where you will be ... You are, where you were" and I didn't understand any of it.

I mean "You were there where you will be ... You are where you were" didn't fall in line and I was super confused.

The words kept haunting me and I didn't know what more to interpret.

I decided to take a break and move out. I opened my eyes and realized how much I desire this to be known. But then I thought who would truly trust me, so I decided to remain quiet.

Apparently it turned out to be a big news in the world news and everyone was shocked and began to imagine it as a proof of UFO. It clearly wasn't the case, but I had to remain quiet.

One night, we were at the bar when my friends looked at me staring at the news and they jumped in and asked "Who do you think .. it is…?" "Now would you want to go to the Mars?" My friends continued joking around when I saw the woman again. She was wearing a black coat and had white hair walking down the street like she was heading towards me.

I decided to run for I didn't want to be around her and move to Mars. But I guess it was too late for she had entered the restaurant already. I opened the door for her and told her "I am not going to talk to you anymore … I need to leave and forget about me and all."

She held my hand and looked into my eyes with deep stare and told me "Do you know what they are going to do? They are going to bomb Mars and who is responsible for this… You and me!! I can't let this happen to Mars. Mars was my home and I have lived years to see human going there and beginning a new life for the planet deserved better than Matons…"

"Matons?? What is that?? Who are you?? Oh my god… you are not from here… you live on Mars … why did you pick me? Why did you get me into this? You messed up Mars and now you wanna mess me up 'cause I like Mars??" I panicked and I didn't know what to say …

"Listen to me... Matons are people from Mars ... They were the best species on Mars million of years ago. They believed that earth was primitive and believed in spiritual and religious stuff. But then came a time when we wanted to live the lives like you, but it was too late. Our technology had taken over us so much that we didn't have the means to survive the menace of technology. And we were doomed then."

She held me and added further "I survived for I saw you talking to your mother about going to Mars and I thought you would understand?"...

"Well I was talking to my mother 3 days ago... What bullshit are you giving me?" I interrupted.

"Listen, If you wanna believe me... know this that I had seen future and I saw you... I am coming from my past to the future of universe which is your present." All of this will complicate things ... why don't you get up and come with me" She looked at me staringly.

"I can't leave my mother ... she loves me and I can't be there to fulfil your fancies... you seem weird to me... Look at you ... you are trying hard to be Meryl Streep from Devils Wears Prada or Kamala Harris in one of the DNC debates I saw weeks ago... Go away... you don't belong here anyways ... how the hell are you roaming freely... it's a democratic country for it's citizens and not invaders!!!" I was panicking.

"Well here is what I will do then. I will wake your mother up and this will all end... your desire to be on Mars ... I will take you to Mars and then leave you there so that before she gets up you are not back..." She threatened which didn't make any sense to me...

I looked at her suspiciously!!!

"Mom, wake up ... its 12pm already and you need to take your medicines." My sister woke my mother up.

"Ohh no.. what did you do? I didn't even see if Violin reached Mars or not. She will leave him there .... Ohh god what did you do? Now how will Violin return ... you could have waited for few more minutes I don't know what to do now. Let me go to sleep again... I will try to see what happened" My mom woke up sweating in the dreams.

"WHAT .....THE HELL ...ARE YOU TALKING ABOUT?? Violin ... Mars... Woman... are you crazy ??... I mean how could you even go to the extent of thinking all this? This is one of the weirdest dreams you have ever mentioned to me. You should sleep on time."

My sister was surprised and left from the room.

My mother was still in panic and she tried sleeping again but couldn't.

"Oh my god, how will Violin now return to earth? He is alone.!!" My mother kept complaining and began crying. She was worried for me and she told my sister "I hope Violin is safe in Mars. Can you check the news and figure out if they have reported anything?" My mom continued her saga.

"Mom Stop!! What are you talking about? Was it a dream? Why would Violin go to mars he is at his home? I just spoke to him." My sister got irritated.

"Was it a dream? But Violin was telling me that he is going to Mars"

My mother looked confused.

My sister asked my mother about what I had mentioned to her over the phone last night.

She narrated the whole conversation to my sister.

So apparently, my mother and I were gossiping about things when I abruptly told my mother that I plan to enroll for a program by Nasa (which was a lie) and that I would begin training in a month's time for my trip to Mars.

My mother was scared, and she argued "No we will not go. We don't want to go. I didn't want you to go to army when you wanted as a kid and now you are asking to move to Mars!!"

I began teasing her further "Imagine mom your son creates history and helps begin new life on mars .. His name will be written in glorious terms and will be remembered as a name in the world. You should be proud of your son. "

My mother looked convinced and worried "What do you think of yourself? Who is going to take care of me? Why would I let go off my son? What has country given to me... there is nothing left for me... I don't want to give anything to the country. I will not let you do it.!!"

"But I have done it already and I have registred you too to travel" I added further masala to non sense conversation.

"WHAT!!! I am not going anywhere... how will my dialysis happen? I have my kittis and tea parties... I have to go to goa and there is no water on Mars. We will not survive... I don't want to die... Just deregister yourself and me." My mother was in absolute shock and was giving in to my nonsense.

"What about dad?" I added to her misery.

"Well dad is sleeping, and he will never leave earth. How will he flirt on Mars...? Besides now I have some 450 friends on facebook. Internet won't work so no video call with my sister. I am getting old ... nobody will take me or your father. He is only going to gossip even in the plane and Mars" My mother didn't leave the chance to take a chance on my dad.

My sister laughed at my mother's narration and went off to sleep. My mother was anxious and went to her room.

Few hours later, my mom heard my sister screaming and crying.

She had woken up telling my mom that Violin is still on Mars.!!!

"LIFE IS FULL OF SURPRISES"

"BEING SERIOUS IS INJURIOUS TO HEALTH."

Morning Blues

It was a surprise visit and I boarded the plane

I was in the queue when I looked at the view

He was checking the tickets, I checked him all the way

There were 6 people between him and me

I counted each one going away

Every time one moved ahead, I tried making the contact

My eyes were dialing but his eyes were checking the tags

The more closer I got to him

I saw him and his clearly

The dusky beard the perfect butt

The muscle popping shirt the oozing lips

The cute hardworking face

The early morning-work kinda demeaner

I wanted to volunteer to raise his fever

2 more to go and I finally looked into his eyes

He saw me asking him for the paradise

But poor boy was duty bound

I hid my ticket to earn more face time

I was almost closer when his little loose shirt

And perfect edged chest made me weak in the early morning haze

I looked at him he looked at me

I smile he smiled I handed over the ticket

He checked and checked every field

And his eyes did the talking and he returned the ticket
I opened my bag to keep my ticket
I needn't do this but I needed it anyways
I wish I could go back and let him check me one more way
I walked slow steps I walked close to him
I took a deep breathe and his body smell made me moan
With my chest wanting to grab him in the bay
I knew I was gonna chicken out
I moved ahead with my short lived romantic date
And I walked ahead waiting to enter the plane
I boarded and sat when he walked close to me
My eyes followed him moving from the left to right
I asked for some help
Even he knew it was an idea out of shelf
He held my hand to help me put my luggage up
The luggage weighed 4 kilos and he couldn't stop smiling
I pretended it was heavy, but he knew what was heavier
He asked me if I need anything more
I abruptly answered "You don't wanna ask me this"
he blushed and looked around and went away
I knew he wouldn't dare do anything
I knew it was a miracle I was praying today
He asked me if I wanna buy something
And that he could give me at the counter someway
I picked it up from there and asked if I could see whats on the tray

He took me at the back while the rest of crew were busy serving

I took a left and he took a right

We both looked at each other and had a flying bite

He walked from right to left shaking his head for challenging me

I began holding my breath and breathing heavily

He held my hair and kissed me gently

He kissed me gentle deep and then rough all the way

I so wished I could drag him somewhere

Or even jump to make out all the way

He kept kissing me while holding my hands at the back

I was now worried if his playmates come

But I guess he had mapped them anyway

And then he stopped after a bite

And I couldn't believe that just happened

I opened my eyes and quietly walked towards my seat

When he spanked me and held my butt

Did he mean something more?

Or did he mean he won the war

I lost all my guts but my gutt felt under played

We didn't talk much after that

Until when I decided to deboard, he responded

Thank you for choosing us; fly us again

I took my card and shook his hands

Pasting it on his palms and rubbed the index on the palm

He blushed again and his smile made me crazy

I looked down and walked towards the door
His beautiful and notorious smile
Paced the way for my day

...And I Didn't Stop Loving Vegas

This is what I did before I jumped...

I guess this was called Disney replica.

I had a little moment with this bird... She understood me more!!

And some more...

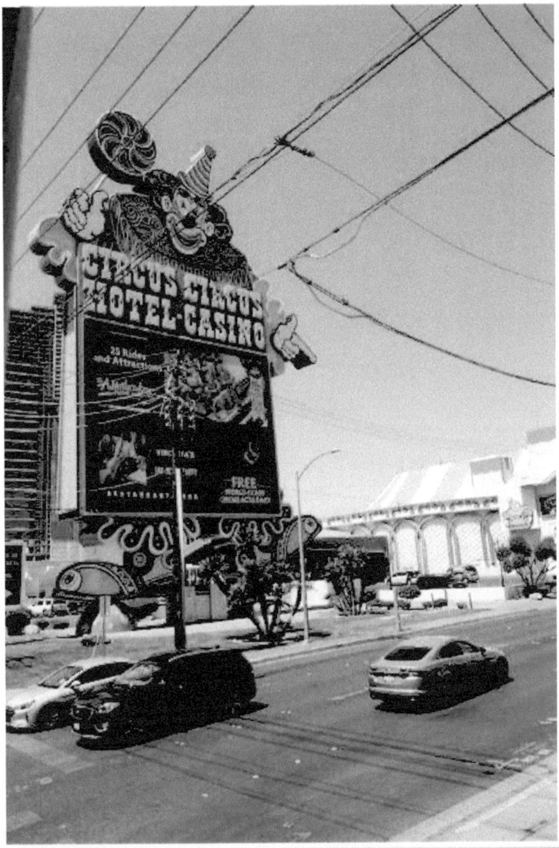
CIRCUS CIRCUS
HOTEL-CASINO
25 Rides and Attractions
FREE

MGM

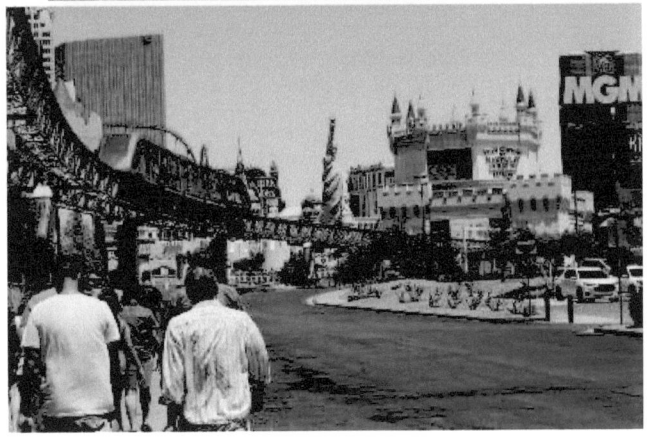

THE KID WITHIN YOU IS ALWAYS ALIVE. IT'S THE ADULT YOU WHO CHOOSES TO SUPRESS IT.... NEVER LET THE CHILD WITHIN YOU DIE... IT'S THE ONLY THING THAT CAN LET YOU FEEL ALIVE.

That's Love for old time sake

I survived on this.

The Golden garage

Don't you worry hun!!

Paris returned!!

Ceasar

This Ceasar looks sexy!!

I don't know what it was .. some strange ships.

And then life changed!!!

Not The Usual Way

After finishing his class from School, Gatian left for coffee in a restaurant close-by. It was sunny afternoon and the restaurant was empty; perfect for Gatian was tired of back to back classes in his school. His supervisor shouted at him for he entered a class late.

Gatian was a tall handsome teacher and a lot of people used to stop him to talk to him just to get a glimpse of him.

That day, a student stopped him and asked irrelevant questions and he was late because of that.

He was very irritated and wanted to just run away. The principal asked him to extend for another period the next day for the rulebook said that the teacher needs to give another period in-case of late entry to a class.

He never liked the rule book and the principal who made it.

In Tel Aviv, he was relatively new to the city.

His sabich was ready and was served on his table. As soon as he was about to eat it, his phone blinked;

It was Tzuriel's message;

"דְתוא וְייזל הצור ינא? התא הפיא!" (Where are you? I want to fuck you!)

He responded "אובל לוכי אל ינא. רפסה תיבב ינא!" (I am at school; I can't come)

Tzuriel texted "תוקד 30 דועב דלצא דתוא הארא!" (I will see you at your home in 30 minutes).

Gatian took the sabich along and paid in haste and ran. He was scared he could be called out by his neighbors if he didn't reach.

He took the bus close-by and ran towards his home. His heart was beating for he knew that Tzuriel could get adamant sometimes.

He reached his home in 15 minutes and went directly to the washroom for shower. It was sunny and he was very tired already.

He undressed himself and stood under the shower. The moment the water touched his body, he felt refreshing and relived. He moved his hands towards his chest and rubbed his hand to feel his nipps. As much as Gatian feared Tzuriel, he desired him as much. He began imagining what would Tzuriel do to him the moment he would come. He moved his hands towards his butt slowly with the flow of the water and held the butt and pressed it hard.

Gatian filled his mouth with the water lifting his head up and kept wiping his face to let him feel the drops hitting his face.

He picked up the towel and dried himself and it was 45 minutes already and there was no sign of Tzuriel.

He came out of the shower and wore his boxers.

He went to the kitchen to see if he had milk for coffee and realized that he didn't. He walked through the entire house waiting for Tzuriel and sat on the couch to rest.

In few minutes, he went off to sleep.

Hours later, he woke to realize that Tzuriel hadn't come and he hadn't called either.

He felt strange for Gatian was under the impression that Tzuriel was already on the way.

He felt hungry and walked towards the kitchen. He lifted the pan and put it on the gas to make some omellette and suddenly the door bell rang.

He knew it could only be Tzuriel at this time. He opened the door and it was Tzuriel. He hugged him tight and said "I am sorry, I needed to drop Asa to the airport for her flight got delayed and I couldn't have come then.

םימעפל דושחל הלוכי איהש עדוי התאש הווקמ ינא.(I hope you know she can be suspicious sometimes).

"Well if you think she would feel suspicious, why don't you tell her?" Gatian teased him.

"Tell her what?? What I am gonna do today to you?" Tzuriel played along.

"Well, I don't know what you gonna do but I am very tired and I just want to sleep" Gatian added the fire.

"Only if I let you...." Tzuriel responded and held Gatian in his arms.

Tzuriel was a tall dark alpha male kind; he had his beard and dimpled cheeks teasing Gatian. Tzuriel had little hair that always used to arouse Gatian.

Tzuriel looked into Gatian's eyes and pushed him to the wall. "Watchout, it a mirror at the back!!" Gatian reminded.

Tzuriel pushed him and took him to the wall near the door and kissed him tightly. They both began kissing each other with the temperature soaring high. Tzuriel pulled his hair and lifted his face and licked his eyes. He began kissing again and they both began rubbing their body with eachothers.

Minutes later, Tzuriel moved his hands through his navel and dived into his boxers and held his dick.

Gatian moan a little and Tzuriel didn't waste a minute and went down to suck him.

Gatian couldn't hold himself and pulled Tzuriel's hair while he was sucking him. He kept moaning and feared that he might cum but didn't let Tzuriel stop.

He had his eyes closed and breathing heavily when Tzuriel began licking his balls and slowly sucked them. Gatian couldn't handle it and pushed him a little and Tzuriel turned him around and bit his butt.

He went for his hole and began licking him. Gatian's body was not able to handle and he hit his hands hard on the wall with Tzuriel moving his tongue.

Suddenly Gatian screamed; for Tzuriel bit him at the hole. He hit his fist on the wall in pain and pleasure. Tzuriel looked at his eyes and smiled . Tzuriel's huge body covered Gatian's leaner body and held his nipples while kissing his neck. Tzuriel couldn't stop himself and in few seconds he inserted his dick.

Gatian moaned heavily but Tzuriel kept humping in heavily. Gatian could sense every muscle in him of him and began calling out Tzuriel.

"Ohh My man.. Tzu…. Give it to me…" Tzuriel kept fucking him near the wall.

They both moved to his bed. Tzuriel lifted his right leg and stretched it up to insert.

In few seconds, Tzuriel was in and began dripping in. Gatian looked right where he could see them in the mirror and him moaning while Tzuriel was kissing his chest.

He then lifted his both legs and inserted immediately.

"You know I like this … You know I wanna fuck you like this everyday!! I am not going to stop tonight until I know I have made you beg for me more. I so love you Gaz and I love fucking you." Tzuriel said this and bit his lips.

The whole bed was moving and Gatian could see it through the mirror and told Tzuriel to not stop at all.

Gatian spanked him from behind and began pushing his butt in. Tzuriel's butt was heavy and tight and everytime Gatian spanked him, He would bite Gatian and fucked harder.

"Put all in me. Keep doing it ... I want you to do this every night with me" Gatian kept talking.

"I will... Tonight Gaz!!!" And Tzuriel lifted him and took him to the kitchen.

"Not in the kitchen, we have to eat after this!! It will be uncomfortable" Gatian told Tzuriel.

"Stop talking and move up" Tzuriel lifted Gatian through his butts and began putting his dick in. He moved forward and bit Gatians nipples. He kept sucking them and bitting so hard that Gatian couldn't stop and had cum.

"Look even you liked it" Tzuriel looked at Gatian while he continued fucking him.

"Asa doesn't even know how to handle it... Its boring with her. You are mine forever and no one else. I will fuck you everyday."

"Harder Harder Harder.. Pls !!" Gatian didn't hear anything and only asked for more.

Later, they went to the washroom under the shower and began cleaning themselves.

"You are mad. You didn't stop and didn't cum either." Gatian said.

"Don't worry I will cum... And I will cum in you for sure." Tzuriel responded.

"Yeah right! Clean yourself!" Gatian smirked.

They both ate the food that Tzuriel had ordered already. It was falafel and Gatian's favorite sabich.

They both went to the bed and laid down.

"Asa will come tomorrow so we have the night for ourself." Tzuriel mentioned.

"What did you tell her?" Gatian moved his head on his chest and asked.

"She doesn't need to know. She is in the flight right now." Tzuriel ignored the need.

"I am sure the neighbors would tell her that you didn't return." Gatian asked.

"I hope you know that I stay in a new building where my neighbors are 2 kms away. Nobody else!! Nobody!" Tzuriel clarified.

"Then why didn't you call me at your place. Nobody would have known." Gatian asked.

"What do you mean? I just thought you were closer to your home and I was planning to drive closeby anyways for some work." Tzuriel questioned.

"I mean I want to sleep with you everyday every night. I really loved what you do to me but its like temporary." Gatian added.

"You mad! You know the people around. This is Tel Aviv... It's a new and modern city but seeing a guy with a married man isn't yet normal view to have. Besides you like it because its not everyday. Asa and I respect each other, but we don't feel with each other. It makes things normal and then boring. If you and I had sex everyday, do you think we would enjoy it any longer. NO!! And I don't want to kill that fire within us. Asa and I are just husband and wife; I feel more connected to you. And in our structure, we can only get what we have.

The moment we would try to add more to it, we will lose it." Tzuriel added.

Gatian didn't say anything and just kissed Tzuriel. He kept quiet but wanted more of Tzuriel.

"I hope you know that I love you. I just met you after Asa so we just make peace with it. I desire your body, but I desire your soul more. You are a beautiful man and I don't desire anyone else. I am happy and content with you." Tzuriel saw the questions in his eyes and tried reassuring.

Gatian moved his hands around his chest and responded, "I love you too". "But.." he whispered slowly and kissed his chest.

They both hugged each other and went off to sleep.

Gatian woke up and ran for his school for he didn't want to be late. Tzuriel told him that he would stay at his place and they could go for the movie close-by later.

Gatian finished his school time while he was very anxious and asked Tzuriel to meet him near the cinema close to his school.

Tzuriel didn't want to disappoint him so he reached 15 minutes earlier. Gatian called Tzuriel and told him to enter the auditorium and that he would see him soon.

It was a romantic movie and Gatian entered a minute before the movie could start. He sat close to Tzuriel when he held his hand and put in a ring on his wedding finger.

"Look I can't marry you the way world wants it ... But I do want you to know that this is special for me and I do want you in my life for life so this is the best I can do to you for I know you deserve to have the ring on your finger and I don't want to loose you whatsoever. So, if it means us exchanging rings, this is my ring for you, and I love you more than you know Gaz." Tzuriel smiled and kissed Gatian.

Gatian couldn't believe what Tzuriel did. He looked into his eyes and moved closer to ears and whispered "I Do! As much as you Do!!" He had tears in his eyes for he had never imagined he would have a ring on his finger.

He teased Tzuriel by moving his hand around his zipper and said " You don't know what I am going to do to you today!!! Be ready for it. Tzuriel Ahaz.. You are gonna see the wild of me, your husband"

"I am ready for forever and I want you to do me as much as I would do to you today. I love you my soul" Tzuriel kissed Gatian and looked into his eyes.

They both held each-other's hands and saw their first movie as a married couple.

SOME RELATIONSHIPS ARE BEYOND THE NORMS OF THE WORLD

www.ingramcontent.com/pod-product-compliance
Ingram Content Group UK Ltd.
Pitfield, Milton Keynes, MK11 3LW, UK
UKHW042002230426
12048UKWH00009B/487

9 789353 479480